LIVIA WAS BATHING
IN A WOODLAND STREAM . . .

She stared into the pool and then froze with horror for, in addition to her own face, she glimpsed another, half-obscured by the leaves of the tree. It was a man's face, bearded and ugly . . .

"Wot's the matter, little lady? Didn't mean to startle ye." His voice was as horrid as his appearance. "Come out . . . I want to see ye again . . . all of ye."

Seeing him step closer to the edge of the pool, Livia found her voice and screamed loudly.

"Sir Justin, help, help meeeeeeeee," she shrilled frantically, praying that he was awake . . .

Other Novels By
Zabrina Faire

Lady Blue
Enchanting Jenny
The Midnight Match
The Romany Rebel
The Wicked Cousin
Athena's Airs

Published by
WARNER BOOKS

EC A

Your Warner Library of Regency Romance

BOLD PURSUIT

Zabrina Faire

WARNER BOOKS

A Warner Communications Company

WARNER BOOKS EDITION

Copyright © 1980 by Florence Stevenson
All rights reserved.

Cover art by Walter Popp

Warner Books, Inc., 75 Rockefeller Plaza, New York, N.Y. 10019

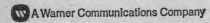 A Warner Communications Company

Printed in the United States of America

First Printing: December, 1980

10 9 8 7 6 5 4 3 2 1

BOLD PURSUIT

One

A fresh spring breeze, which succeeded in lifting several tall hats from the heads of gentlemen pawing in the street below Miss Livia Pemberton's bedroom windows, also caught at her dimity curtains. Billowing out like sails, they were captured by another vagrant zephyr and, turning to thin streamers, followed it through the window.

"Lawks," Nancy, her abigail, exclaimed inelegantly, and throwing down her dustcloth, she bent over the sill to retrieve the offending draperies and was in imminent danger of also losing her mobcap to those harrying winds. Clapping a protective hand to her head, she bounced back, hastily banging the casements shut. "It do seem more like March," she complained to Miss Pemberton, who was seated at her small French writing desk, tapping a quill pen reflectively against her chin.

"But it is April!" There was an unusual lilt to Livia's voice and that, notwithstanding the fact that several of the notes she had penned were scattered on the floor.

Retrieving them, Nancy reflected that Miss Pemberton was in particularly good looks that afternoon. Her gray eyes, usually so grave and even solemn, were sparkling and there was a definite upward turn to lips which, in the year and a half she had been in her service, smiled but rarely, adding to Miss Pemberton's reputation for weighty thought. Regarding her mistress critically, Nancy wished she would have been permitted to arrange the neat bands of dark brown hair into ringlets similar to those worn by Miss Marianne Semple, Miss Pemberton's first cousin, but as usual, she had been defeated in this wish by her mistress's reminder that "twenty-one is not eighteen, Nancy."

"Nor be it a hundred and twenty-one, Miss," Nancy had quite ached to reply, being of the opinion that Lord Ormond would have appreciated the change. However, she had held her tongue, knowing that Miss Pemberton would never have countenanced such pertness. It was a pity, for, unlike Miss Semple's golden locks, Livia's curls would not have required the application of papers or hot irons. Left to its own devices, her hair would have curled delightfully and it was a crying shame to deflect it from its natural bent.

Nancy stifled a giggle. It was possible that marriage to Lord Ormond would help to free Miss Pemberton's mind of many of her more rigid notions and bring more than smiles to her face. The prospect of that imminent ceremony had already weaned her from her nightly delving into the musty pages of Greek and Latin historians. Furthermore, she had had several new gowns made and three of them were trimmed with bands of lace and ribbons, quite foreign to a wardrobe which, in general, consisted of gowns plain in cut and drab in color.

"Quite as if she was practicin' to be a spinster lady," Eva, one of the underhousemaids had commented.

Though Nancy had angrily refuted this allegation, privately she had concurred with it, fearing that after three London seasons and having turned twenty-one in November last, it was quite possible that Miss Pemberton would find herself in that most unenviable position. Then, like a comet, Roderick Craven, Lord Ormond, had flashed across Miss Pemberton's horizon and within a fortnight the thick, squat volumes beside Miss Pemberton's bed had been replaced by slim books of poetry that Lord Ormond had brought her. Six weeks after that they had become affianced and should have been wed ere now—had not Miss Pemberton's aunt, Lady Maude, after an exchange of letters with her brother, Lord Semple, capitulated to his wish that the two cousins be married at the same time. According to her parent, Miss Semple was on the verge of becoming betrothed herself. Nancy bit down another giggle. It was a situation Miss Pemberton had accepted gracefully enough, though she should not be surprised if

9

her fiancé had not done more than a little champing at the bit, him being so eager to wed her mistress.

Miss Semple, on the other hand, was not at all pleased. According to her handmaiden, Mitzi, she was being coerced into marriage by her father. His choice was one Sir Justin Warre, who, if Mitzi were to be credited, was as rich as Croesus, whoever that was, and over twelve years her senior. He was, in fact, her father's boon companion, which meant that, like Lord Semple, he was an antiquarian. It was an interest which kept the pair of them traveling all over England scouting out traces of ancient Romans—though why they should be interested in people who had been dead for hundreds and hundreds of years, Nancy could not understand. Nor, she was positive, could Miss Semple, who had accompanied them on their last venture into Dorset, returning last night out of sorts and so weary that she had fallen into bed without even partaking of supper. Nancy guessed that, being very lazy, she was probably sleeping yet.

She jumped and threw a hand over her mouth, stifling a surprised squeak, for, at that moment, the door from the hall opened suddenly and Miss Marianne Semple came into the room, slamming the door sharply behind her. Nancy shot a resentful look at her. Did she think the practice of knocking had gone out of fashion? She must have just arisen, for she was still in her nightdress and pegnoir. Remembering her manner and her place, Nancy bobbed a curtsey, which went unnoticed as Marianne came impetuously forward to stand in front of her cousin's desk.

"I must have slept for an age," she announced

dramatically, running her little hands through her mass of tangled golden hair. "Stupid Mitzi did nothing about my curls last night," she added petulantly.

"You fell alseep too quickly," Livia smiled up at her. "I trust you passed a good night, Marianne?"

"Oh, it was well enough," her cousin allowed. "It was a mercy to be in my own bed. The King's Head—the accommodations were not to be believed, my dear. As usual, Papa was thinking of his purse rather than my comfort. Oh, I am so infernally weary of his stratagems concerning money. At least . . . when this miserable knot is tied, I shall not need to resort to such shifts in order to coax a few pennies for my gowns."

Liva's fine gray eyes held some concern as she probed Marianne's gloomy countenance. "I had thought you reconciled to it, my dear."

"I am," Marianne's face suddenly brightened and she seized the ends of her skirts and danced around the room. "Oh, yes, I am . . . I really am!"

"Well," Livia was not particularly surprised at this sudden change of mood, it being Marianne's way. "I am glad of that. You are not thinking of crying off, then?"

"Oh, no, it is better to be wed for . . ." Marianne cast a quick glance over her shoulder at Nancy, who had resumed her dusting. Lowering her voice, she said, "Do dismiss that chit. I am sure her long ears are cocked to catch my every word."

"I doubt it, but, very well. Nancy," Livia raised her voice, "would you be so kind as to fetch us some tea. I find myself thirsty, of a sudden—and you, Marianne?"

"Oh, yes, I should love some tea. Mitzi left

11

mine by my bed and it was horridly cold when I awakened."

"Tea and a few slices of toast, Nancy," Livia ordered.

"Yes, Miss, at once, Miss," Nancy answered respectfully, and curtseying, whisked herself out of the room, wishing she might slam the door as had Miss Semple. She was quite aware as to the reasons for her mistress's sudden hankering for tea. Though she had never liked Mitzi, she being one of those Frenchies, she felt quite sorry for her, having so much blame heaped on her head. Never, she reflected as she went down the stairs, had she ever seen two cousins more dissimilar! And despite the fact that Marianne Semple was lovely-looking, even with her hair hanging in elflocks all about her face, she much preferred Miss Livia, who, if not quite so beautiful, had much the better disposition of the two. She sighed. She would have given a monkey to know what sort of secrets Miss Semple was confiding to Miss Livia.

If she could have, she would have heard Marianne saying, "for if one is wed, dear Livia, one can do exactly as one chooses."

"'As one chooses'?" echoed Livia. "I've never heard that."

"You haven't," Marianne's blue eyes were round, "but you are ever so much older than I, Cousin, and in consequence must have listened to a deal more gosisp—especially in three seasons!"

"'Gossip'?" Livia questioned, not looking at Marianne, mainly because she was annoyed, yet annoyed at herself for being annoyed. She knew that in making reference to her advanced years and her prolonged presence on the town, Marianne was not being spiteful. She was merely stating a fact. However, with a surge of delight, Livia reflected that that fact would cease to be a fact in a fortnight, no, not even a fortnight—twelve days! Only twelve more days intervened before Miss Livia Pemberton would become Lady Ormond. Dear Roderick! She conjured up his face—starting with what had first attracted her—his deep blue eyes, often partially hidden by lengthy burnished gold lashes, which were the same color as his admirably coifed hair—cut a little longer than the present styles but eminently becoming . . .

"If one is married, one may have a lover," Marianne announced.

Her inventory thus arrested, Livia stared at her cousin, " 'A lover'?"

"Oh, yes, that is how it is done," Marianne told her complacently.

"How—*what* is done?"

"Livia, I cannot think you are attending," Marianne complained. "When one is married, one can always have a lover. My friend Edith . . . you remember Lady Sibley, says it is quite easy and no one the wiser if you are careful. And I am sure that she is right . . . because I have practiced."

" '*Practiced*'?"

"Oh, I pray you'll not look so shocked. You see—Papa and Sir Justin were always looking at tracks or whatever and I remained at the inn with a sick headache, only I really was not sick . . . but it is such a bore to walk up hills and get one's gown caught on brambles or to sink in mud searching for bits and pieces of marble or holes where it might

13

have been and, oh, you know, you have an interest in that sort of thing."

"I do . . . because it is interesting," Livia pointed out. "I am sure you would find it so—yourself."

"I am sure I would not. I cannot think of anything more tedious. I hate the country. However, that is beside the point. I was telling you about my headache. After Papa and Sir Justin went off with their guide, I remained in the common room at the inn and such a nice young gentleman came in . . . we had a most pleasant conversation. It quite reconciled me to being married."

"I . . . fear I do not follow you. You conversed with a stranger and that . . ."

"Heed me, Livia," Marianne exhorted her cousin impatiently. "I spoke with him and I could see he liked me and was wishing to know me better. I wished the same thing . . . but, of course, I did not encourage him overlong. I told him I had the headache, too, and I went to my room. Still, when I am married, it will be different . . . when a young man speaks with me in my husband's absence, I'll not need to fob him off, not if I am discreet. And I am sure that Sir Justin will always be at Papa's beck and call . . . so you see?" Marianne spread her hands.

"This . . . is what you have in your mind at the very commencement of your marriage?" Livia demanded in shocked accents.

Marianne's light laughter echoed through the chamber. "Why ever not? I do not want to marry Sir Justin, but he is rich and will provide me with lovely gowns with which I can attract someone I really do like—more than one if I choose. In fact, being married is far better than being single because I can have *numerous* lovers."

"But that is dreadful!"

Marianne bridled, "It is not in the least dreadful. Marrying Sir Justin was, as you well know, never my design. It is Papa who is infatuated with him because of his knowledge of Roman walls, baths and such things. When he offered, Papa consented immediately and insisted I must, too. I am sure that his wealth also had a great deal to do with it—for Papa will not need to provide me with a dowry. If I had had your dear papa, I should not have needed to sacrifice myself . . . but enough, it is decided. Now do tell me about Lord Ormond. I vow, I can scarce wait until tonight to meet him. Papa says he is a gamester. Is that true?"

"Yes, I expect it is," Livia began and was halted by her cousin's giggling.

"Fancy that you should be wedding a gamester, you who have always looked down your nose at such unintellectual pursuits!"

Livia, feeling less in sympathy with her cousin than she ever had before, said tartly, "That is true, but Lord Ormond has promised that he will cease to frequent White's and Boodles."

Marianne's blue eyes were wide, "You have exacted such a promise from him? He must be in love or . . ."

" 'Or'?" Livia inquired with some hauteur.

"Or nothing," Marianne shruggel. "I have forgotten what I intended to say . . . my head's in such a whirl . . . I am really delighted for you, dearest Livia . . . to think that it happened so quickly! A

15

mere matter of two months! But it is time you were settled down and did not think so much on all those books you read."

"I hope that marriage will not turn me into an illiterate," Livia said tartly.

"Oh, no, nothing could do that, but it should keep you occupied with ... other pursuits, since you are in love." Marianne rolled her eyes and moved toward the door. "I must summon that idiotic Mitzi and have her roll up my hair if I am to appear to any advantage at all tonight. Those old cats at Almack's are so particular. By the way, if you have any curiosity concerning Sir Justin, he will be there tonight. I pray he'll not glower and stand against the wall with folded arms when I dance with other gentlemen. Oh, dear, I do wish I found his appearance more to my liking ... I expect I shall have to spend *some* time with him—once we are wed."

"Gracious, you speak as if you were bound to wed a veritable Caliban."

"A what?"

"A monster."

"No, he is not precisely that ... but when I mention the word 'precise,' he is that ... precise, neat ... and he dresses in black like a parson ... with no feeling for the mode at all and ... oh, you will see for yourself and I shall meet your intended and pray you've made a better choice than I, which I am sure you must have, since I was not at liberty to choose." Marianne whirled through the door, stopping for a second on the threshold to add, "I can hardly wait to hear what you will say. I think you'll not be so disapproving of me, then!"

Once she was freed from that volatile presence,

Livia felt a great relief and, at the same time, a certain depression of spirit. She drank the tea Nancy had brought her and ruminated on her situation. Unintentionally, she was sure, Marianne had made her feel old and also ill-prepared for the glorious event which had filled her thoughts ever since Lord Ormond, with the moonlight turning his golden hair to silver, had said soulfully, "My dear, my very dear, my adored Miss Pemberton, dare I hope that you will be mine?"

She had heard him with ecstasy, realizing at that moment the reason for her Aunt Maude's knowing looks all that day. Of course, Lord Ormond had been most correct, applying to her aunt, who was, in effect, her guardian, before breathing a word of his feelings to her. To Livia, who had dreamed of his Lordship ever since they had met at a subscription ball at Almack's, it had been almost a miracle. She had had many offers, of course, but they had come either from fortune hunters or from men who did not please her. She had never expected that one so handsome, so eligible, so brilliant would have come her way. Generally, she found that gentlemen, especially those aged twenty-three, which was Lord Ormond's amount of years, did not appreciate a female with any pretensions to learning. As one of her governesses had once cautioned her, "I should like to draw your attention to that sentiment expressed by a dean of St. Paul's: 'A little wit is of value in a woman much as we value a few words spoken plain by a parrot.'"

It had been an observation which had infuriated the young Livia, imbuing her with a desire to prove that misogynistic clergyman wrong. Loftily, she had retorted, "I intend to wed a gentleman who will appreciate me for my wit rather than for the lack of it."

The governess had smiled wanly and held out ten ringless fingers, "I once cherished that very hope myself, Miss Pemberton, and a forlorn one it has proved to be."

Livia, looking at the woman's thin, hawklike features, narrow eyes and slit-mouth had nodded, withholding the obvious rejoinder. However, years later, Miss Livia Pemberton, attractive, charming, neat of figure, light on her feet as any dancer and with a fortune of ten thousand pounds a year had found to her chagrin that her appearance and her fortune had attracted only those gentlemen with pockets to let. Others, when quizzed as to the philosophy of Descartes, the writings of Montesquieu and Aristotle's *Poetics* as reflected in the Greek dramas and in the works of Racine and Corneille, had looked at her blankly, then with horror, hastily quitting her side to seek the company of less erudite damsels. Livia had remained undaunted.

"I shall not change my approach," she had told a protesting Aunt Maude. "I take after my father."

"You cannot remember your father, since he died when you were but a year old—He never recovered from the death of your mama at your birth," Aunt Maude had retorted with a reminiscent sniff.

"You've said he was determined to die and did it. You've also told me that he was a fine scholar. I have his determination and his learning. I was not meant to sit in a corner to sew a fine seam and be bored."

"It is only too true that you cannot sew a seam

fine or otherwise—but if you are not careful, Livia, my dear, you'll end up an old maid."

That conversation had taken place toward the close of her first season. Variations of it had been repeated during her second. Then, in her third when both she and her aunt were close to giving up hope, she had sighted Lord Ormond across that crowded dance floor at Almack's. She had been so taken with his appearance—tall-and-well-built-wearing-his-evening-clothes-magnificently—that when he had desired a waltz of her, she had been almost reluctant to put him to the test.

Yet, like her father before her, she was true to her convictions. She was also only too aware that even the most handsome of faces could pall were there not a lively intelligence behind it. Consequently, once the waltz had ended, she took a deep breath and posed a favorite question, "Have you read *The Eumenides*, my Lord?" It was a query that had stopped many a burgeoning conversation and left more than one gentleman gaping at her in dismay—but not Lord Ormond.

"Bless you, I have," he answered eagerly, "though I cannot say that I care much for the Orestean trilogy."

"Oh," Livia, who had warmed to the first part of this sentence, had felt an ominous throb in the region of her heart. She primed herself for the usual disappointment as she asked, "And why not, my Lord?"

"I shall tell you . . . but first, should you care for some ratafia?"

"That would be very kind," she answered dolefully, recognizing the question as a ploy he had instituted to tactfully remove himself from her side. Much to her surprise, he returned and as she was sipping the drink, he said, "You asked why I did not care for the Orestead. In my opinion, Orestes seems a poor sort of fellow. Electra did his thinking for him. I much prefer Oedipus . . . a bit wrong-headed, true, but I cannot believe he deserved his fate."

"But he *did*." Livia could not help replying in spite of her governess's oft-repeated admonition that gentlemen value agreement above argument. "He had a hasty temper and an impulsive disposition. He knew the prediction that he would kill his father and marry his mother—consequently, he rushed out of his supposed parents' house without so much as a by-your-leave and when he met that old man at the crossroads and had that argument over the right of way, he killed him, not realizing it was his father. Then, when he met Jocasta, a middle-aged widow, he did not hesitate to marry her."

"But, Miss Pemberton, consider, by solving the riddle he had caused the Sphinx to slay herself and stood to gain a kingdom. Furthermore, he had no notion that he was adopted!"

"If he had possessed an inquiring mind, he should have guessed. If an oracle had told me that I should kill my mother and marry my father, I would think twice before encouraging the attentions of any gentleman over forty."

"You would have more reasons than an oracular warning to prevent you from taking such a step, Miss Pemberton. However, though I am not so sure I am in agreement with you on Oedipus, I shall think of what you have said when I reread the plays, as I try to do at least once a year. Meanwhile,

I pray you'll not think so poorly of me as to refuse me another waltz—you are uncommonly graceful, you know."

It had been the beginning of a friendship which had rapidly developed into a romance. Aunt Maude approved, for she, too, had capitulated to Lord Ormond's charms. "Such address, my love," she had practically purred, "and not a fortune hunter. I have made inquiries from the most unimpeachable sources and I hear that he numbers among his friends none other than Lord Alvanley and Mr. Greville. I do hear that he is overfond of gaming but I am assured that he is well able to support this habit. Too, he has been uncommon lucky. Still, I wonder, dear child, if a week is long enough for us ... er, you ... to form an opinion?"

Livia, reading a manuscript written in Lord Ormond's flowing Spencerian script, and reveling in his admirable use of the language as revealed in a poem dedicated to herself, could say ecstatically, "Oh, yes, Aunt, he is all I have ever dreamed of encountering."

The meeting had been doubly fortunate, since it had taken place at a time when her enchanting cousin Marianne was out of town visiting her friend Lady Edith Sibley at her estate near Brighton from whence she had been bidden to join her papa and Sir Justin in Dorset. Their stay had been extended, the town still emerging from winter's snows.

Livia shuddered. It would have been most unfortunate had they appeared together at that ball, for there was no doubt but that Marianne took the eye, and in this, her initial season, she had never looked more ravishing. Indeed, at the two balls they

21

had attended before her departure for Brighton, Miss Pemberton had felt more like a chaperon than a participant as the gentlemen had massed around her cousin. It was amazing that Marianne presented so romantic and bewitching an image, when, of a truth, she was so very hardheaded. Still, she did feel a trifle sorry for the girl. It could not have been pleasant being forced into a marriage one did not desire and to a man as reportedly dull as Sir Justin Warre and all because Uncle Henry was too miserly to provide a dowry. Yet to enter into such an alliance with duplicity in mind could not augur well for the future—particularly if Sir Justin were as difficult and jealous as Marianne had hinted.

Livia felt a twinge of sympathy for the man. It was quite possible that just as the handsome and poetic Lord Ormond was her ideal, the beautiful Marianne Semple was Sir Justin's. Under such circumstances, she could feel more than a mere twinge of sympathy for him—being wed for his riches rather than himself. It was a damnable situation and one which she had fortunately eluded—but by such a narrow margin! Her eyes, which had been clouded with concern for poor Sir Justin, cleared as she thought of dearest Roderick, whose fortune equaled her own—to think of him was to bring chin to cupped palms and elbows to desk, to look impatiently at the small china clock on the mantelpiece and mentally urge it to tick away the hours more quickly—so that it would be night and she would be at the ball in her fiancé's arms.

The small but brilliantly lighted rooms at Almack's were, as usual, crowded with a handsome and well-garbed group of the ton. Livia, looking very well in a demure blue silk gown trimmed with silken floss at its modest neckline, stood at the edge of the floor watching Lord Ormond dutifully whirling her cousin through the measures of one of the more popular German waltzes. Marianne, who had appeared extremely impressed by Livia's fiancé, looked exceptionally attractive—her hair curling charmingly, her cheeks delicately flushed and her eyes bright. That the décolletage of her white silk gown had raised the eyebrows of those stern patronesses Mrs. Drummond Burell and Lady Sefton seemed not to trouble her. She gave every evidence of enjoying herself thoroughly.

Shooting a glance at Sir Justin Warre, standing a few paces away from her, Livia's lip curled. Her incipient sympathy for his possible cuckoldry had vanished practically at first glance. It was not his appearance, she told herself. Though she did not care for swarthy complexions and hair so dark as to appear blue-black, he was not ill-looking. If he were two or three inches shorter than dear Roderick, his figure was well proportioned and he carried himself well—too well, she decided. He stalked rather than walked, his chin was held high and it was only too obvious that he was insufferably proud, looking about him with the disdain of a prince faced with a passel of commoners. Not even the Regent had ever seemed so full of horrid self-consequence! Livia had the definite impression that he had taken a dislike both to her and to Lord Ormond and at first glance, too! It was also possible that he did not even like Aunt Maude—having exchanged no more than the briefest of pleasantries with her. It had not occurred

23

to him to follow Lord Ormond's gracious example and demand that Miss Pemberton be his partner for the waltz. On relinquishing Marianne to Lord Ormond with the barest of bows, he had stood glowering at the pair and had even neglected to fold his arms. Livia flushed and looked away hastily, for at that moment Sir Justin had turned his frowning gaze upon her.

Self-consciously, she fixed her eyes on the dancers and was not a little disconcerted to find that Marianne and Roderick had disappeared. Just as this unsettling fact registered, Sir Justin, moving closer, said curtly, "It seems as though we are deserted, Miss Pemberton."

"I think not," she returned. "Marianne probably wanted a whiff of fresh air. It is uncommonly warm this evening, do you not agree?"

"No, ma'am, I do not believe it to be warm at all," came the uncompromising response.

"Well, even so, I think you will not need to repine—my fiancé has claimed me for the next dance and . . . ah!" Livia smiled triumphantly as Marianne, clinging to the arm of Lord Ormond, came across the floor to them, energetically waving her small ivory fan and smiling at her resentful swain.

"I vow," she breathed, as she joined them, "waltzing is monstrously exhausting—I was quite, quite breathless and felt I must faint if Lord Ormond did not procure me a glass of wine." She raised grateful eyes toward him, "I cannot understand why you are not more tired, my Lord."

Lord Ormond's golden lashes descended over his smiling blue eyes, "I cannot say that I was ever wearied by dancing, particularly when I am matched with so graceful a partner as you, Miss Semple or as you, my dearest Livia."

Livia smiled and let a tiny sigh of relief slide through her lips. She had been, she realized, holding her breath in anticipation of she knew not what? Seeing her intended and her cousin side by side, both so blue-eyed, smiling and golden, she had been seized with alarm—even though she had told herself that with her nuptials so near, she was a fool to worry. However, she had but to hear Lord Ormond address her as "my dearest Livia" to realize that her fears were groundless. Though Marianne was a flirt and quite capable of trying to entice Roderick, there being no doubt but that she had been taken by his appearance, it was obvious from his attitude that he was being no more than polite to her—as became one who was soon to become her cousin by marriage.

"This waltz is ours, is it not, my love?" Roderick had moved to her side. Now, taking her arm, he put an end to her ruminations.

"Of a certainty, it is," she assented. The smile that Livia flashed in the direction of Sir Justin contained a quotient of triumph. Unfortunately, he did not see it, his eyes being fixed on Marianne's vivid little face quite as if he would mesmerize her with the intensity of his dark gaze. Much as she did not like him, Livia once more felt some sympathy for him. He would never be able to be as sure of his bride as she was of dear Roderick. Nor would Marianne ever be happy as the wife of a scholar. From a tiny child, she had resisted all lessons save French, a language she had laboriously conned because of a desire to visit Paris once hostilities were at an end.

Since Napoleon was now safely restrained upon the island of St. Helena, Livia was positive that Marianne would soon be persuading her bridegroom, her father's cavils notwithstanding, that rather than visiting Rome with him as their guide, they must honeymoon in France. Nor would Sir Justin have the opportunity to seek out the monuments and the museums which she knew must interest him. Instead, he would be accompanying his willful and determined young bride to dressmakers and jewelers'. Her thoughts were again dispersed by Lord Ormond's whirling her about and then pulling her toward him, his brilliant eyes fixed on her face. Meeting his compelling stare and by it rendered infinitely surer of her place in his affections, Livia could ask bravely, "Did you enjoy your waltz with my cousin?"

He shrugged, "Well enough. She has a light step but, I fear, my dear, that she has an even lighter head. I cannot say that I admire females who giggle endlessly over naught." He looked uncomfortable, "But I fear I have said too much. I hope you'll not chide me for my frankness, my dearest Livia. I know she is your close relative."

Livia was fully aware that she ought to protest but caught between duty and inclination, she yielded ecstatically to the latter—every cobwebby fear banished. "Oh, dear, I expect you must be entitled to your opinion even though I cannot concur with it. Marianne is quite charming when you get to know her," she lied.

"You are the most generous of women," he gave her one of his soulful looks.

Livia blushed and turned away—thus obtain-

26

ing a brief glimpse of Sir Justin with Marianne in his arms. She was amazed at the change in his expression—gone was his frown. He was gazing ardently down at Marianne and, obviously, his whole heart was mirrored in his eyes.

"Oh, dear . . ." Livia sighed.

"What did you say, my love?"

"Nothing," she replied and meeting her fiance's questioning blue gaze, she forgot all about what must surely be Sir Justin's rude awakening.

Two

After eight days of glorious sunshine, the changeable month of April became intermittently rainy. Any hope that it might clear by high noon of the fifteenth—the day on which the double wedding of Miss Livia Pemberton and Miss Marianne Semple was due to take place—was blasted by an ominous gray dawning and a sky which grew grayer and more ominous by the hour. By the time the clock chimed eleven, Lady Maude, standing on the threshold of Livia's chamber resplendent in a silver satin gown which blended admirably with her snow-white hair, was saying with an anxious glance at her gleaming skirts, "I anticipate a squall, I really do." Her kind face crumpled. "Oh, dear, I was so hoping it would be a sunny day ... Henry's rheumatics—

he'll be on edge and, well . . . 'happy the bride,' you know, child."

Livia, sitting at her dressing table while Nancy added the finishing touches to her high coronet of braids, smiled at her aunt's lugubrious reflection. "I, for one, could not be happier."

"You look very happy, my love," Lady Maude agreed. "And I am pleased that Marianne has prevailed upon you to wear white. It is a most becoming gown. Indeed, you will both be as pretty as . . . as princesses."

"Marianne will be the princess and I shall be taken for her attendant," Livia smiled wryly. "I happen to believe that white is a little trying for one of my years."

" 'One . . . of . . . my . . . years'?" her aunt repeated incredulously. "Wherever did you get that foolish notion?"

"My governess . . ."

"Miss Sims!" Lady Maude exploded. "I should have dismissed the creature years earlier had I but known she was filling your head with such arrant nonsense, fluttering about the schoolroom like a huge black bird of ill omen. Marianne complained about her so consistently that I listened in on her chatter and was never more shocked—envious cat! And you so vulnerable and naive—nor have you changed. Imagine making you feel as if you were on the shelf if you were not wed by eighteen and a half. It is utterly ridiculous. Why I . . ."

"Was wed at seventeen and a half," her niece reminded her.

Lady Maude flushed, "Even so . . . those were different times and you favor your dearest mother and Henry agrees with me that she was the beauty of the family. Furthermore, you look every bit as young and as pretty as Marianne—prettier, for you are not pulling a long face and sniffling."

"Oh," Livia's expression turned anxious. "Her mood remains the same, then?"

Lady Maude nodded carefully, not wishing to upset her elaborate coiffure. "She'd be out of place at a funeral," she said tartly. "Such prattle about 'burnt offerings' and 'sacrifices' on the altar of 'parental tyranny' has put me quite out of patience with the chit. Yet, it has seemed to me that until this morning, she has been in tolerable spirits—as much as I have seen of her, I mean. I wonder if it is not Lady Edith who has put this bee into her bonnet. I have always considered her a bad influence on Marianne and they have been together so much this past week."

"I cannot say—since my acquaintance with Lady Edith is but minimal. It is possible, however, that the enormity of the step she is about to take has been brought most forcibly to her mind this morning," Livia lowered her voice. "I cannot say that I should look with equanimity upon wedding that man."

Lady Maude closed the door behind her and moving further into the room she gave her niece an anxious glance, "You may be quite right, my dear. Though I would never say as much to Marianne, I cannot understand why Henry holds Sir Justin in such high esteem. He seems a man of few graces and I find his disposition, indeed his general deportment, very surly. I cannot help but think that Marianne might have been more in sympathy with one nearer her own age—though, of course, fortunes such as Sir Justin possesses are not to be found growing wild throughout England."

"True . . . and thirty's not precisely ancient," Livia found it necessary to remind her aunt—her own thirtieth birthday being a scant nine years in the future.

"Thirty that acts like thirty and not a dour fifty . . . though I cannot admire the excesses to which some men of fashion will go—to appear in browns and blacks like a schoolteacher or, as Marianne says, a country parson, seems to me very odd and . . ." Lady Maude broke off impatiently. "It is far too late to refine upon such matters. Though I cannot say that I have ever regarded Marianne as highly as I have you, my dear, I do want her to be happy. I certainly hope that Henry is right in his contention that marriage with Sir Justin will mold her character."

"Is that what Uncle Henry believes?" Livia inquired doubtfully, the while she saw Nancy making odd grimaces which, on glimpsing the abigail's dancing eyes, she recognized as a worthy attempt to stifle her laughter.

"It is indeed," Lady Maude returned, "though from my own experience, I have never found such hopes to be realized. However, you know that your uncle Henry is uncommon stubborn and he has quite set his mind on this match."

Livia nodded. She was weary of this particular discussion. In her present state of euphoria, it was very difficult to dwell upon her aunt's worries, her uncle's stubbornness and stinginess and her cousin's dilemma when, in a little more than a hour, she would be addressing Roderick, Lord Ormond, as "husband." She had not seen nearly enough of him in the past week—he having been in the country readying Ormond House near Melton Mobray in Leicestershire for her reception. "I want my own beloved to see it at its very best," he had told her with one of his soft blue looks, "since it is there we shall be spending the first weeks of our married life."

Livia sighed and glanced at the clock. As usual, it seemed to be ticking all too slowly.

Lady Maude with rare perspicacity said, "I expect I have wearied you with this dwelling on your cousin's woes. Do forgive me, my child. I'll leave you but first let me assure you that I have never seen you in such looks." Blowing a kiss to Livia, she quitted the chamber.

"She be tellin' you no more'n wot's the truth, Miss," Nancy enthused. "Though I do wish you'd've let me comb your 'air into ringlets."

"No curls, Nancy. It's not my style. Even Roderick has said so." With a certain pride, Livia continued, "He has told me that he deplores frivolity in females."

"Umph," Nancy moved toward the chair on which lay Miss Pemberton's long veil. "If your aunt can wear ringlets, I cannot see . . . but no matter." She had the veil poised over Livia's head when the door was flung open by Marianne, making one of her tempestuous entrances. Her last, thought Nancy, noting with a measure of satisfaction, Miss Semple's reddened eyes. She did look ravishing though, dressed in shining white, with her golden hair curled and arranged to the best of Mitzi's considerable ability. Nancy, not acquitting Miss Semple of malice aforethought, stepped aside as the girl came to stand beside her mistress, staring at her tragically.

"Dearest, dearest Livia," she cried, "oh, you do look splendid. I cannot go through with it—I must not, it would be too, too dreadful."

Livia stifled an impatient sigh, "Marianne, dearest, you have had all this week to change your mind about Sir Justin, but on your wedding day, it's impossible."

"I know . . . but, oh, my dear, I do not like him. We are not at all suited. I was aware of that from the beginning and of late I am become doubly aware of it. I should only be doing him the greatest disservice in the world, for I believe him to be entirely enraptured with me. He'd not fail to be terribly disappointed once he learned that . . . oh, I know it is all wrong . . ."

"Marianne, you are talking wildly," Livia snapped. "While I cannot agree with the plan you divulged to me when you came home . . ."

"Nor I," her cousin interrupted. "It would be too cruel. I do not want to be cruel to Justin or . . . or to anyone. Yet to make two people suffer needlessly and forever—that would be cruel, also, do you not agree?" She stared at Livia with a strange intensity. "You must agree."

"Yes, but . . ."

"Oh, I knew you would . . . Livia, whatever happens, I pray you'll not think too harshly of me. You have a noble spirit and a sweet nature. Oh, Livia, I do love and revere you as well." Marianne's eyes filled with tears.

"Marianne." Rising, Livia took her by the shoulders and actually shook her, "It is too late to change your mind. You cannot do it."

Marianne stared at her. "Too late, is it? Then, I shall not, but you must remember what you told me. Let it be on your head, Livia, whatever happens." Moving away from her cousin, Marianne dashed out of the room.

"Well, I never!" Nancy gasped, and meeting Livia's eyes, stuttered, "I . . . I am s-sorry, Miss, but s-she . . ."

"I quite understand, Nancy. Poor girl, she is sadly distraught. I pray that I have been able to make her see where her duty lies."

"I expect she will, Miss," Nancy shook out the veil. "This be beautiful, this veil."

"Perhaps I should warn Aunt Maude . . . oh, I do hope she does not contemplate anything rash. She did speak so wildly!"

"Beggin' your pardon, Miss, but it might just be a case of the nerves. My sister Liz was that het up afore her weddin', but she calmed down wonderful in church. Now she'n him are as snug as two bugs in a rug."

"You do cheer me, Nancy," Livia smiled.

She was, however, feeling nervous as she descended the stairs to the hall—but, on seeing Marianne, her veil in place, standing next to her father and Lady Maude and looking quite composed, Livia breathed a sigh of relief and hastened to greet the tyrannical parent.

"Good day, Uncle Henry," Livia smiled and curtseyed.

Lord Semple, a tall, grizzled man of sixty with

sharp gray eyes and a thin-lipped mouth, regarded his niece approvingly, "Well, well, my dear. You look slap up to the mark!" He glanced at his sister. "Dare say I'll be much envied, coming into church with two such beauties on my arm."

"Oh, Papa," Marianne actually giggled.

Livia looked at her cousin in considerable surprise. She had thought that Marianne must strive for composure in the presence of her father, but she had not expected such a display of dramatics. With a twinge of annoyance, she wondered if perhaps Marianne was showing off for her sake. It occurred to her that this was the last time they would need to be together and, with some surprise, she found herself regarding that pending separation with considerable pleasure. Perhaps for the first time in her life, Livia admitted to herself that though they had been together since Marianne was eight and her mother had died, she had never really liked her young cousin. However, she quickly banished this revelation as unworthy of the day.

A rumble of thunder startled them all. "Oh, dear, "Lady Maude cried. "I fear it will storm and soon. I do wish it had been a fair day. As I have always said, 'happy the bride that the sun shines upon.'"

"Poppycock," scoffed her brother. "Come, it's time we were off."

The colonnaded portico of the fashionable church, St. Martin-in-the-Fields, would normally have been crowded with well-wishers, for though neither bride had chosen to be attended by other than their Aunt Maude, with Lord Semple to give them away, both enjoyed a wide acquaitance among the ton and it was well known that Marianne's marriage plans had broken the hearts of several young gentlemen. However, Lady Maude's fears had been realized and the thunder had been followed by a drenching rainstorm. Consequently, Livia and Marianne, alighting from Lord Semple's coach and escorted by umbrella-bearing postilions, came up the steps onto an empty porch. However, the presence of numerous post chaises and barouches suggested a well-filled interior.

"Hurry, my dears," Lady Maude urged as she hastened inside. Livia followed, with her cousin close behind her, but as Marianne reached the door, her friend Lady Edith, a lively redhead of nineteen with bright mischievous green eyes, quickly seized her arm, saying, "Marianne, a word if you please."

"What's that?" Lord Semple, following his daughter, rasped. "We've no time for chitchat."

"Please, Papa, I shall not be a moment." Marianne looked up at him beseechingly. "The fact is I am planning a surprise for Dear Justin, and Edith is aiding me."

"A surprise? What manner of a surprise?"

"You will know in due time, dear Papa. Please . . ."

Looking down into his daughter's lovely face, Lord Semple appeared to soften. "Very well, Puss, but no more than a moment, mind you."

"But . . ." Lady Maude turned back. "The ceremony is due to begin . . ." Her words fell upon emptiness as Marianne followed her friend. "That wretched Edith . . . I pray Sir Justin will put his foot down when it comes to that friendship," she muttered to Livia.

Livia did not reply. She was past thinking about her cousin. Despite the darkness of the day and the corresponding dullness of the stained-glass windows, she found the interior of the church beautiful and welcoming. She smiled happily. All her life, she had attended services here. She had also attended the weddings of numerous friends, some of whom she saw sitting in the pews. Now, she was going to join their number and perhaps in a year or two she would be bringing her firstborn child to be baptized at that marble font. Her eyes grew misty as she looked down the aisle to the altar where she and Marianne would soon stand beside their respective bridegrooms. She shifted her gaze to the third finger of her left hand, adorned now with the pearl and diamond betrothal ring that, Roderick had told her, every Ormond presented to his bride to be. Soon another heirloom would shine beneath it—his late mother's wedding band. There had been moisture in his eyes as he had spoken of his mother. He had said, "I wish she might have been present to see me wed. I know she would have taken you to her heart as have I, my beloved."

Livia sighed and pressed her hand against her cheek. Her thoughts dwelt briefly on his mother. Perhaps she was gazing down upon them from heaven. Addressing that possible presence, she mouthed silently, "I will be a good wife to him. His happiness will always come first with me." She started slightly as a gust of wind caused the windows to rattle. The storm was evidently increasing but she did not mind. She did not miss the sun at all . . .

Suddenly, all thoughts were swept from her mind as behind her, she heard a most fearsome yell. Incredulous, Livia whirled around to find her uncle, his face empurpled to the point where it seemed as if he must topple over in a fit of apoplexy. He was holding a piece of notepaper which he was thrusting at Lady Maude. "READ THIS!" he shouted.

"What . . ." Livia began, aware now of a buzzing in the pews. Glancing behind her, she found that a number of people were staring at Lord Semple while others were craning their necks, evidently striving to understand what had occasioned such an outburst. Then, there was a loud gasp and close upon it a heavy thud. Turning back, she found that her aunt Maude had swooned.

"Milady . . ." an usher was hurrying to her side.

"Damn and blast it, woman," bellowed Lord Semple, glaring at his fallen sister. "Up with you. There's no time for that now with Marianne . . ."

"Marianne . . ." Livia whispered. Something must have happened to Marianne; in her mind was her cousin's wild talk not an hour since. Circumventing her prostrate relative, she stepped to her uncle's side. With one trembling hand at her wildly beating heart and another on her uncle's rigid arm, she said through stiff lips, "I pray you'll tell me what has happened, Uncle Henry. Has Marianne d-done something d-desperate?

"Aye, 'desperate,'" he cried. Looking down at her, he paled and in a lower tone of voice, he added,

"That wretched pigeon's bound for Gretna Green."

"For G-Gretna G-Green?" Livia stammered. "With whom?"

Lord Semple paused. Then, slipping an arm around her waist, he said, "I pray you'll not follow the example of my sister, girl. I would I need not to tell you ... but there's no evading it. My daughter's eloped with your bridegroom."

The rain pelted against the windows of the large traveling coach. Through the storm, the occasional yells of the postboys mounted on two of the four mettlesome steeds that pulled the coach, drifted back to its occupants, of which there were also four. Nancy, huddled in a corner and deeply regretting she had not joined the other servants in offering so many preliminary and, as it turned out, premature toasts to the bride and groom, stole a glance at her mistress's stony face and wished she might offer her a bit of comfort—but even if she had not been too queasy to speak, it would hardly have been her place, and after all, what could she have said? She pressed her hot forehead against the glass and prayed that they would soon come to an inn. Sure they could not drive much longer! However, on seeing Lord Semple, seated next to his niece, she was by no means convinced of that. His Lordship was in a dreadful taking! His rage surpassed even that of the wronged bridegroom, who sat so silently beside her. She stole a glance at Sir Justin and looked away quickly—aware that she had been mistaken concerning the quality of his anger. His dark eyes were glittering and his mouth was so grim that

40

had he been confronting the two malefactors, she was sure he must tear at least one of them limb from limb.

Liva, aware of Nancy's commiserating glances, was grateful that she had not put her sympathy into words, thus sparing her the necessity of answering them. She could not have spoken. She looked dully out of her rainstreaked window into the dimming landscape. She guessed that it must be close on eight and wondered how far they had progressed in the last six hours. The coach was light and well sprung and with her uncle's famous matched grays to pull it, she was sure that in spite of the steady downpour they must be miles from London. More specifically, they must be miles from St. Martin-in-the-Fields and that fashionable assembly which had been present to witness and record the debacle of her hopes, her plans, her happiness. Gossip being what it was, everyone in the Polite World must now know that Miss Livia Pemberton, spinster, who was to have been wed at high noon to Roderick Craven, Lord Ormond, yet remained Miss Livia Pemberton, while her spirited young cousin, Miss Marianne Semple, aided and abetted by her best friend, Lady Edith Sibley, had fled to Gretna Green with that same faithless lord.

How had it come to pass? She bit down a mirthless laugh. No need to search for explanations. She had one in Marianne's letter—a communication she had perused so often that she could repeat it word for word. Closing her eyes, she envisioned Marianne's all-too-clear copperplate handwriting:

Dear Papa:

I know that this missive must come as a great shock for all concerned, but there is no help for it; you must understand what has taken place.

Lord Ormond and I are in Love. We knew it directly we met at Almack's on that never-to-be-forgotten Wednesday. We have seen each other often in the last days and each time our hearts have beat as one. Yet we had all but decided to Honor our Obligations— then, at the last we could not endure the thought of so Cruel a Separation.

Though our actions will seem Reprehensible to you, to dear Livia and to my Intended Bridegroom, believe me when I say it is all for the Best. We cannot knowingly let four people Suffer Needlessly. Consequently, after much painful Searching of our Two Souls, we have eloped to Gretna Green—there to become One. By the time you receive this communication, we shall be on our way north. I beg you will not endeavor to impede us as it would serve No One. Dear Papa, I pray that in time you will forgive your Loving

Marianne.

Once more Marianne's wild words of the morning flashed into Livia's mind. They were all explained. Furthermore, the little nagging doubt that she had not known she possessed until that fateful hour was also clarified. Now that she pondered on it, she was aware that Roderick's excuses concerning his absence from town had never rung true. Though she had not admitted it to herself, she knew full well that he could have instructed his housekeeper to oversee the preparations for her reception. He need not have been there. He had not been there. Instead, there had been clandestine meetings with her cousin —oh, how could he have acted so cruelly, so dishonorably?

Yet, thinking on Marianne's numerous charms, it was all too easy to understand why he had fallen in love with her at first sight. However, as Livia knew only too well, her cousin's enthusiasms were short-lived. No less than four smitten gallants had found that out this season! Roderick would be so hurt! Livia ground her teeth. He deserved to be hurt. He had acted in a thoroughly disgraceful manner—"villainous" was how Lord Semple had described it. Lady Maude had said very little. When they left her, she was in a state of utter prostration —one that she had fully expected Livia must share.

"But I am not prostrated," Livia muttered to herself. "I am furious!" Glancing up, she saw Sir Justin sitting across from her and quickly looked down again, shuddering as she recalled his drained white face and blazing eyes as he had thrown down Marianne's letter.

Retrieving it, Lord Semple, striding out of the church, had thundered, "I am going to fetch her back, never fear. I shall leave within the hour."

"And I with you," Sir Justin had averred.

"And I!" Livia had cried.

"You?" The two men had stared at her incredulously.

"Impossible," Sir Justin had exclaimed.

"Quite impossible, my dear," Her uncle had echoed. "A female has no place in . . ."

"I tell you, I am going," she had interrupted. "I know that she has enticed my Roderick . . ."

"'Enticed' your Roderick'?" Sir Justin had glared at her, "If there was any enticing to be done, that cur . . ."

"Be silent, both of you," Lord Semple had rasped. "Very well, come with us, Livia. I expected you deserve to witness their punishment—for I shall stop this match if I must needs slay the pair of them." He had actually shaken a fist at the heavens and, since they had been standing on the edge of the portico, he had drawn it back glistening with water, causing him to shake it once more, adding, "And damn the elements, I vow we shall be the first to reach Gretna Green. Come . . ." he had gestured at the array of coaches below. "We'll not halt until we are across the Scottish border!"

Of course they had halted—three times to be exact: once to deposit Lady Maude at her home and to allow Livia to change from her bridal attire into a gown suitable for traveling as well as for Nancy to hurriedly pack a handbox and clothe herself in other garments. They had halted a second time at Sir Justin's lodgings for similar reasons and their last stop had taken them to Lord Semple's house where he, too, had changed clothes and ordered the substitution of his grays for the horses originally harnessed to the coach. Consequently, it had been a teeth-clenching, nail-biting two and a half hours before they had swept out of London bound for Coventry or as close as they might approach that town before nightfall. Lord Semple had described a route which led through several counties and covered a distance of some three hundred thirty miles.

Though the journey had seemed fearfully long to Livia, her uncle had assured her that with all the changes of horses he meant to procure at various posting houses along the way, they should reach Gretna Green in four days' time. Four days and they would be in that infamous place where marriages were performed, Scottish fashion, without parental consent, without licenses, simply by the exchanging of vows before so-called reputable witnesses. Livia winced. She had been told many an anecdote concerning those witnesses or "priests," as they were called. Grubby, drunken illiterates, who might formerly have been pedlars, soldiers, blacksmiths or even thieves, they would, for a few coins or even a pint of whiskey, join couples together in "Holy Matrimony." Holy! It was a travesty of all that was beautiful and sacred! The very thought of such an unhallowed ceremony was repugnant to her. Livia put a hand to her throbbing head and hastily took it away to clutch at the strap. Fortunately, she was in time to prevent herself from sliding to the floor at Sir Justin's feet. It was a bad road; it was getting dark and soon they must stop.

She did not want to stop. She wanted to drive fast, fast through the night. She longed for a pair of Mercury's winged sandals so that she might fly to Lord Ormond's side and ask him why ... why after his fervent protestations of love, his eager wooing ... but did she need an explanation when she thought of Marianne, beautiful, spoiled, wanting? Roderick had never been the prime mover in this regrettable proceeding—of that she was certain. No, it had been Marianne. Marianne, who with her lovely eyes drowned in tears, had no doubt told him of her father's coercion and cruelty. Marianne, who, casting him in the role of knight-errant, appealing to his poetic soul, had cleverly manipulated him. It had happened before. More than once, Livia had seen a friend wrested from her side by Marianne's devices. There had been Cynthia, who, a season back, had been on the point of inviting Livia to spend several weeks at Bournemouth with her—but it was seventeen-year-old Marianne who had gone and Cynthia, turned surprisingly cold toward Livia, had never proffered an explanation. She had been too proud to demand one and though she had regretted the loss of her friend, it had not been irretrievable. But Lord Ormond . . . why could he not have seen that Marianne's airs and graces were all a sham, hiding a mulish determination to have her own way?

"All a sham . . ." she whispered bitterly.

"I beg your pardon?"

Startled, she looked up to meet Sir Justin's dark glance. "I was not addressing you, sir." she said.

"Oh? Excuse me. I had the impression you had spoken."

Livia recoiled. He was looking at her as if he hated her. She wondered at his ire. Even in the midst of her misery, she could spare some pity for him who, in common with herself, had been spurned, cast aside and was, by now, a laughing-stock, an object of derision as cuckolds or near-cuckolds must always be. She swallowed a sob. It was too dreadful. It was unreal. She felt almost as if she were in bed and dreaming the whole of it. *Dreaming*. She had dreamt of this day for so long . . . such happy dreams, each ending with her going off in a carriage with her beloved husband. Her lips twisted. She was going off in a carriage—but the dream had turned into a nightmare, for beside her sat a seething uncle and across from her a gentleman whose hot eyes seemed to be shooting sparks out at her.

"We'll halt at the White Lion outside of Rugby," Lord Semple suddenly growled.

"So soon?" Sir Justin's frown deepened.

"We can go no farther tonight, but tomorrow we shall make up for it," Lord Semple assured him. He added, "Trust me, my boy, we'll catch up with them and when I get my hands on that wench, she'll rue the day she was ever dropped from her mother's loins!"

"'Tis no fault of hers," Sir Justin rasped, his eyes once more on Livia's face. "She's not the first of your family to fall victim to the blandishments of a practiced villain!"

Livia bridled, "Nothing of the kind..." she began.

"Hush, I say," Lord Semple commanded. "We've trouble enough without these storms."

Obediently, Livia subsided, but on glancing at Sir Justin's lowering brow, her incipient pity for him vanished. Once again, she was convinced that she had never met so unpleasant a man. Reprehensible as Marianne's actions had been, she could not blame her cousin for seizing any opportunity to escape him. But not with Roderick...oh, my God, not with Roderick...She turned aside to stare into a mass of darkening trees which should by now be lining the approach to Ormond House. The sigh that went through her was weighted with woe. She had often heard her aunt say "I wish I could die." It was a favorite but entirely meaningless expression, for

Lady Maude loved life. Livia, however, could find a depth of meaning in the phrase. Fervently, she wished that some manner of cataclysm might overtake her and put a period to an existence which would never be anything but utterly, utterly miserable. She sniffed and sniffed again, fumbling in her reticule for a handkerchief and then stared stupidly down at a large white square of linen that had been shoved in front of her. Raising drenched eyes she encountered Sir Justin's hard stare.

"Take it," he commanded brusquely, "I cannot abide vapors!"

Livia was moved to retort, "I am not indulging in vapors. I . . . I . . . " to her consternation and embarrassment, her voice broke and more tears flowed down her cheeks. Snatching the handkerchief from its donor, she buried her face in its capacious folds, thinking ungratefully that he was perhaps one of the most unpleasant men it had ever been her misfortune to encounter. The prospect of spending four days in his company was suddenly so horrendous that she began to wish she had taken her uncle's advice and remained in London—but that would never have answered! She cast a glance at Sir Justin, but for once he was not looking at her—he was staring out of the window and it seemed to her that she discerned a moistness in his own eyes. A twinge of pity for what he must be suffering went through her and then vanished. He would have been in worse straits had her cousin decided to wed him. It was not he who was to be pitied, it was dear Roderick, whom she could not hate—no matter how hard she tried. It was very confusing and suddenly she was very tired of the jouncing carriage and the uncongenial company. In spite of the need for haste, she was actually glad that they would soon be stopping at an inn and she relieved of having to look at Sir Justin for the rest of the evening!

Three

Toward midafternoon of the next day, Lord Semple, sitting rigidly on his side of the coach as he had sat all the previous day, looked out of the window and said with some satisfaction, "Remarkable time . . . remarkable. . . ." His acerbic glance rested on Sir Justin's closed face, then flickered toward Livia. "We'll reach the border ahead of them, never fear. Spend the night in Wigan—then on to Preston . . . ought to reach Gretna Green midmorning, day after tomorrow."

"We've gone fast," Livia commented dutifully, knowing that that was what he wanted to hear.

A gratified smile quirked up the corners of his mouth, "Ormond'll have no cattle can equal these. A night's rest and they were as fresh as when we brought them from the stables yesterday. Of course we'll need to hire a new team once we reach Wigan."

Yesterday. Livia's teeth clicked together as the coach hit a depression in the road. She clutched the strap tighter. A night and the better part of a day had passed since yesterday, but if she closed her eyes, she was back in the church with her uncle's sustaining arm around her waist and his eyes furious, yet concerned, as he confided to her that terrible news. That moment seemed frozen in her mind and with it were other equally dismal impressions. They occupied all her thoughts. In the five hours they had been on the road, she supposed they had made good time but other than they were headed due north, she had no idea what towns they had passed or where they were. She was wearying of dwelling on her misfortune but it was impossible not to wonder, to speculate, to endeavor to understand how Marianne had managed to snare Lord Ormond. Livia did not believe her note—could not believe that it had been "love at first sight," as she had termed it. Perhaps there had been some attraction but, undoubtedly, the flame had needed some fanning. In that endeavor, Marianne had, of course, been abetted by her dear friend Lady Edith, a notorious madcap, who saw nothing amiss in encouraging Marianne to appropriate her cousin's fiance. She winced. She had always disliked Edith, who, in turn, had made it abundantly clear that she considered Livia dull, staid and proper, which, she thought drearily, must be true—at least according to Edith's standards.

Other than her insistence that a woman had as

much intelligence as a man and should be allowed to exercise it, she had never chafed at the other restrictions society had placed upon her conduct. It had never occurred to her to steal out to masked balls in such forbidden haunts as Vauxhall Gardens or the theaters or to arrange clandestine meetings with swains of which her Aunt Maude had disapproved. Marianne, on the other hand, in her brief months in town, had not hesitated to disobey her aunt's strictures in all regards. She was a born rebel. Livia flushed, remembering confidences concerning stolen kisses—familiarities that she had never encouraged not even from Rôderick. A chaste salute to the cheek was all she had ever allowed—while Marianne ... She shrank from contemplating the other images now crowding into her mind ... Marianne locked in his arms Marianne standing with him at the altar exchanging those binding vows which she had once expected to make ... no, no, no, it could not happen. Even if she, Livia, could never call him husband, Marianne must not be allowed that privilege, either. She had no right ... she ... a shattering jolt halted her rueful cogitations. The coach rocked back and forth and suddenly the door beside her swung open. Her grasp wrenched from the strap at her side. Livia felt herself falling forward and out. In that same moment she was aware of someone falling against her—she felt wetness and hardness and then they were both rolling over and over down a grassy slope while, behind her, the horses neighed, men yelled and a woman screamed loudly.

When she opened her eyes, Livia was looking up at a tall tree. Portions of her body were aching, her elbow was smarting and she felt unpleasantly wet all over. For a vague moment she regarded the trees' dripping branches, trying to understand what had happened. Then, aware that she was lying flat upon the ground and that various stones were pressing against her or she was pressing against them, she raised herself slowly and was startled to see that her gown was raked up above her knees and that there was a long red scratch on one of her white lisle stockings. Just as these unpleasant facts impressed themselves on her consciousness, she heard a cough and saw that Sir Justin Warre was just getting to his feet. With a gasp, she pulled down her gown.

Meeting her flustered gaze, he moved toward her, rubbing a hand against his forehead and saying with something less than his habitual calm, "Are you hurt?"

She took a moment to reply, flexing and unflexing her arms and moving her legs, "I do not believe I am," she concluded. "Are you?"

"No," he rasped.

"I am very muddy, though."

"Yes . . . it's muddy ground."

"W-what happened?"

"I expect that the coach must have hit a depression in the road. I fear it has turned over. You and I were thrown clear."

Oh, dear what of—of Uncle Henry—and Nancy?"

He frowned, "I am not sure . . . I hope . . . they were not harmed but . . . their side . . ." he reached down a hand. "Are you able to walk?"

She grasped his proffered hand and, holding it tightly, she scrambled to her feet, exclaiming as she did at her cloak which was soaked with water and coated with mud. "I must have fallen in a puddle."

"We both did," he said. "Can you walk?"

Still clutching his hand, she took a step forward and then another. "Yes, my powers of locomotion seem unaffected."

A flicker of amusement appeared briefly in his eyes, "As are mine, Miss Pemberton. We are both very fortunate. Let me help you up the incline." He put a sustaining arm around her waist.

Evading it, she said coolly, "No need, sir, I am quite myself, I assure you." Scrambling up the slope, she stopped at the top, looking about her in dismay. The coach lay on its side and while the postboys held the nervous horses, John, her uncle's coachman, was gently lowering Lord Semple to the ground—not far from where Nancy lay moaning in pain.

Looking at her uncle's pale face, Livia said between stiff lips. "He . . . he's not . . ."

"No, damn and blast, but I've broken my leg," Lord Semple growled, proving that he was alive if not well. "And the Lord knows what's happened to your poor wench. Fortunately, we're not far from The Green Man, where we must have halted to change horses. Hugh's gone to fetch help . . . owwwww, careful there . . . you are not handling a sack of grain," he yelled at the coachman, who had just succeeded in depositing him full length upon the sward.

"Oh, I am sorry, Uncle," Livia said distressfully. "Is there anything I can do for you?"

"Yes, you can stop talking to me and leave me alone," he replied ungraciously.

Thus rejected, Livia hurried to Nancy's side. Kneeling down, she asked, "Are you in much pain, child?"

Nancy raised tear-filled eyes, "I . . . my arm . . . an' my 'ead . . . I 'ad a shocking blow when we t-turned over. Oh, Miss, was you 'urt, too?"

"Not at all."

"Oh, Miss, I am glad . . . I thought when I didn't see you . . ." More tears ran down her cheeks.

"Shhhhh, you mustn't talk." Livia brushed the girl's tangled hair back from her pallid face. "Just lie still. My uncle tells me help will be coming soon."

"Oh, Miss, you are that good . . . 'tisn't fair . . . 'tisn't wot 'appened today. 'Twas monstrous cruel . . ." she moved and then she groaned and clapped her hand to her shoulder.

Sir Justin came to kneel beside Livia, "Is she badly hurt?"

"Her arm broken or wrenched and her head . . . I wish I had something to give her . . . I cannot believe hartshorn would suffice."

"No, Miss . . . do not trouble yourself . . ."

"Shhh . . ." Livia said gently.

"I have brandy." Reaching into the pocket of his greatcoat, Sir Justin brought out a little silver flask and, pushing back the top, he handed it to Livia.

"Thank you." Taking it, she tipped the bottle toward Nancy's lips, "Drink this, my dear. 'Twill make you feel more the thing," she urged.

Obediently, Nancy swallowed, "Oooh, it do burn." She blinked up at Livia, her eyes full of concern, "Miss, what will 'appen now?"

"I cannot say." Livia replied ruefully.

"You won't never catch up wi' them." Nancy mourned.

"There's where you're mistaken, my girl," Sir Justin's tone was grim. Rising, he said decisively, "I assure you that one of us will catch them."

Two hours later, Lord Semple, ensconced in a large chamber on the second floor of The Green Man and having submitted wrathfully to the ministrations of the doctor called in to set his leg as well as attend to Nancy's badly wrenched shoulder, was in a state of impotent fury. He had just learned that a certain harried young couple had not only changed horses at the inn that very morning but had commandeered the whole of the stable, thus preventing any possible pursuers from hiring a fresh team. The roars that escaped his Lordship at this intelligence had rattled the rings on the bedcurtains and made the ewer jump in its basin.

"That wretched little minx," he growled. "'Twas her notion, I've no doubt. Well, she'll not profit from this scurvy trick. The stage to Preston comes here later this afternoon. You take it, Justin, my lad, and I'll give you monies to hire another post chaise once you've arrived. You should reach Preston in the morning."

"You'll not need to fund me, my Lord," Sir Justin had told him. "I've enough to see me through and shall board the stage, never fear."

"Eh..." Lord Semple had looked relieved at Sir Justin's remarks concerning money, but his face had clouded almost immediately. "What I would not give to go with you..." he slammed a fist against the bed and groaned as the mattress shook.

"Were I to put hands upon that wench . . . I charge you . . . bride or no bride, I want the wench brought here and . . ."

"I shall do my best to return her to you, my Lord."

"I pray you'll not be soft with her." His Lordship had stared at Sir Justin suspiciously.

"I swear I shall not. But it's well you sleep now. I'll be gone ere you wake, but I'll send you word from Preston."

"From every stop along the way, if you please."

"If it be possible, my Lord, I shall do as you ask. You may be assured as to that."

"Damn and blast this cursed leg!" Lord Semple fumed. "No matter . . . you, too, must try and snatch some rest. There's no telling what discomfort must await you on the stagecoach. Drove one once on a bet. Wouldn't ride in one, even for a bet. Off with you, now. You've my blessings for this venture."

"I thank you, my Lord," Sir Justin gave him one of his grim smiles and, bowing, strode from the chamber. Livia, a silent witness to the exchange, now moved forward.

"Uncle . . ." she began tentatively.

"Well?"

"I . . . wish to go with him."

"You?" her uncle repeated incredulously. "Nonsense."

Meeting his angry stare, Livia lifted her chin, "I've as much right as he. It was my bridegroom Marianne stole and . . ."

"Enough!" her uncle interrupted. "From all accounts your abigail will be laid up at least a week. A young, unchaperoned female cannot go jaunting about the countryside with a man to whom she is not even related."

"B-But we . . . we could s-say we were cousins . . . we almost were . . ."

"But you are not and all the world knows that you are not. If word were to reach London, and such word always does, you would be hopelessly compromised. No, your place is here, my girl. Sir Justin will do well enough without a female to plague him."

"But . . ."

"*Still* you persist," Lord Semple moved restlessly upon his pillows and winced. "I am amazed, utterly amazed that you should even suggest such an undertaking, you, a gently bred young woman with what I have always imagined to be more than your share of common sense. I think you must have fallen on your head and injured your brain . . ."

"I assure you . . ."

"Please . . . no more. Leave me, I need to sleep."

Livia sighed, "Very well, Uncle. I am sorry . . ."

"And so you should be," he grunted. In a somewhat softer tone, he added. "I know that this has been a great shock to you, my dear, but I have faith in Sir Justin. He'll not disappoint us. You do not know him as I do. He's an extremely tenacious young man and he did love the wench, may perdition seize her!"

Tears pricked Livia's eyes as she emerged from her uncle's chamber. Near her in the corridor, a casement window faced the road which wound north to Preston, to Lancaster and ultimately to

Carlisle, which lay only eight miles from the Scottish border and Gretna Green.

Moving to the window, she stared out indignantly. For once, the rules governing feminine behavior seemed unnecessarily binding and even ridiculous. She was an intelligent, mature, resourceful person and, at twenty-one, well able to fend for herself. A man of her years could wander wherever he chose and none to raise a question, while she must needs remain behind bound to the inn for want of a female companion! She chafed at the prospect. Unlike Lord Semple, she had little faith in Sir Justin's ability to deal with Marianne as she deserved. Despite his brave words, she could well imagine that he would once more fall victim to Marianne's practiced blandishments and end by cosseting her cousin and challenging Lord Ormond to a duel.

"No," she whispered. "It must not be."

Yet—what could prevent it? In less than two hours' time, the stage would stop to take on passengers and leave almost immediately. Turning her gaze from that distant road, she stared moodily down into the courtyard of the inn. Her glance fell on Hugh, the postboy, who was evidently flirting with one of the prettier maidservants employed in the hostelry. Hugh was the coachman's son and at sixteen, he, though small for his age and looking little more than thirteen, could also do as he chose. If he should suddenly decide to board the stage, none could prevent him. For the first time in her life, Livia wished strongly that she had been born a man. Then, her eyes narrowed and smiting her palm with her clenched fist, she ran purposefully down the stairs.

There was no room inside the elderly coach that rumbled into the courtyard of The Green Man toward four in the afternoon. However, there were two places outside. One was taken by a large burly man wearing a high battered hat and a much mended greatcoat over shabby pantaloons stuffed into broken boots. The second was allotted to Sir Justin and then, at the last moment, a beaming and doubtlessly bribed coachman decided that there would be room for a slim boy who had come running out of the hostelry to confer with him somewhat frantically. The lad was muffled in a greatcoat, its collar pulled up high about his neck and he wore a peaked cap shoved down on his short curly hair, its brim shading his face. It seemed as if he were having a little trouble crawling up onto the narrow perch but Sir Justin reached him a hand which, after the barest hesitation, he seized, climbing aloft and muttering his thanks but keeping his eyes fixed on the inn yard. He was waving at a pert and pretty young maidservant but the girl appeared sadly indifferent to his enthusiastic farewells.

"'Tis a good thing he be young 'n thin," muttered the first outside passenger. "Ain't much room up 'ere'n the way we get knocked about goin' over bumps and the like . . . one of us could 'it the ground." He squinted up at the sky. "It do look like rain."

"I expect we'll need to make the best of it," Sir Justin shrugged.

"Eh?" the man peered at him. "You be an odd one to ride out 'ere. Speak like one of the ton, you do. Down on yer luck, pal?"

Sir Justin surveyed him for a moment, his eyebrows raised, his look questioning. Finally, he drawled, "I hardly believe that is any affair of yours, my good man."

The other, flushing an ugly shade of purple, shot him an angry look but on meeting Sir Justin's hard black gaze, turned away hastily. Meanwhile, the boy, clutching the railing, continued to keep his face averted while Sir Justin, taking no notice of either of his two companions, stared straight ahead.

The coachman laid his whip across the back of his team and the cumbersome vehicle lurched forward, its old wooden framework creaking and groaning with the motion of its wheels. In a matter of minutes, they had reached the main highway. The coachman flicked his long whip again and the horses, neighing and snorting, increased their speed. The three outside passengers swayed against each other even though the boy did his best to hold himself as far away as possible from his neighbor.

They had passed three mile posts when a massing of the clouds suggested that the first passenger had correctly estimated the weather conditions. The boy pulled the collar of his coat even higher and darted a nervous glance at Sir Justin, whose eyes were still fixed on the road. His expression was as imperturbable as if, indeed, riding on the outside of a coach were a usual occurrence in his life. Then, as a splatter of drops hit his face, he composedly unstrapped a large umbrella from his portmanteau and unfurled it, a procedure emulated by the first passenger—whose own umbrella, though neither as large or as fine as that used by Sir Justin—sufficed to keep his battered hat from being drenched. The boy merely bent his head against the shower.

"You did not provide yourself with any protection against the elements?" Sir Justin demanded as the rain grew heavier.

"No, sir." The boy's response was low, almost inaudible, "I do not mind inclement weather."

"Serve 'im right, young sprig ain't dry be'ind the ears yet, specially not now 'e aint." The first passenger opened a capacious mouth and laughed loudly at what he obviously considered a witticism.

"You'll catch your death, young man." Sir Justin admonished, tilting his umbrella toward him.

"Thank you, sir," came the mumbled response.

"Ain't got much to say for 'isself," commented the first passenger.

"Possibly," Sir Justin replied in freezing accents, "there are some who have entirely too much to say for themselves."

"Oh, sorry, sir. Beggin' her 'igh'n mighty worship's pardon, sir. I expect your worship . . ." whatever else he might have said was interrupted by a sudden fork of lightning that seemed almost to split the sky asunder, followed by a crash of thunder so loud that it caused the horses to plunge and rear. The first passenger, losing his balance, fell heavily against Sir Justin but jerked back quickly, "Beggin' yer worship's pardon," he repeated with a look far less subservient than his words.

Sir Justin, however, seemed unaware both of

his action and his excuses. He was staring at the boy, who, in that moment had darted a terrified glance at the heavens and in so doing had inadvertently lifted his face from the collar of his great coat. He had looked down again instantly but not before Sir Justin had glimpsed extravagantly lashed gray eyes, which he recognized immediately as those belonging to the young woman who had sat opposite him for the past two days.

"M-Miss," he had started to say and then thought better of it. Instead, he muttered furiously, "What in thunderation are you doing here and in such attire?"

The gray eyes were now fixed upon his face. He read defiance in them as well as an anger that matched and possibly even surpassed his own. The answer was carefully couched in a boy's piping treble, "'Tis my own desire to cross the border, sir. I 'as business wot needs seein' to, same as you."

"Damn you," Sir Justin retorted. "You'll go nowhere save back to your uncle directly we reach Preston."

"Shan't," came the low response. "I 'as as much right to go where I'm goin as ... as anyone."

"And I ..." Sir Justin ceased speaking, for they had started up a steep and extremely narrow bit of roadway, heavily wooded on either side. "Hold tightly to the railing," he ordered. "This is a bad stretch and there's a chance the horses might make a misstep. It could be even more perilous going down the hill." He fell silent again, holding the umbrella over her head, his mouth set more grimly than ever. Inwardly, he castigated himself for not having realized sooner that there was something not quite right about this youthful and extremely self-effacing traveler. At that moment, he was more than merely angry, he was beside himself with rage! Given his way, he could have shaken Miss Livia Pemberton until her teeth rattled, for naturally there was now no question of his continuing on his journey. Once they had reached Preston, he would need to use the post chaise to convey this blasted female back to her uncle!

"God deliver me from puling lovesick wenches," he muttered savagely to himself as he slipped a steadying arm around her waist. They had reached the top of the hill and were descending a slippery and rock-strewn roadway. "Hold on tightly," he repeated and staggered as his large fellow passenger, seeming to lose his balance, fell heavily against him, clutching him about the chest.

"Sorry, sir," the man muttered.

"Watch what you're about," Sir Justin returned and grunted as a sharp elbow dug into his stomach, momentarily robbing him of breath. In that same moment, he felt a huge hand inexorably pushing him back. Taken off guard, he made a wild grab at his assailant, his hand closing on thin air. Then, unable to regain his balance, he fell against Livia and heard her cry out. At that precise moment, the coach lunged forward, sending Sir Justin and Livia toppling to the ground.

The coachman, unaware of anything untoward happening behind him or of cries that were lost amidst the pelting rain, the shrieking winds, the crunch of the wheels as they hit the stones, the neighing and snorting of the horses as they plunged down the hill, drove his team forward and in a few moments the equipage was lost to sight around a bend in the road.

Lying in a thicket, Sir Justin dazedly stared at the place where the coach had vanished. He was aching in a dozen places. Yet his mind told him that though he had sustained a bad fall, he was not seriously hurt. However, the girl at his side might be another matter. It occurred to him that while he had been yelling futilely at that unheeding driver, she had not joined her voice to his. Indeed, she had not made a sound since her first startled cry as that miscreant had thrust them from their places. Fury shook him but he quickly banished it; he dared not dwell on the reasons behind the man's unwarranted attack, not yet. He moved his limbs and, as he had suspected, nothing was broken. A short laugh escaped him as he remembered it was his second tumble of the day and under oddly similar circumstances.

"It's true . . . as she said, I must bear a charmed life," he murmured and then frowned. It had been his grandmother who had made that observation. He did not like to think about her. Yet, as she had in life—so she had in death—asserted herself at odd moments, a persistent spectre who would not be exorcised from his consciousness. "Get thee behind me," he breathed and hated himself for actually casting a wary look over his shoulder. There were times when he could almost imagine she was still with him, just beyond the periphery of his vision, her dark eyes, the exact color and shape of his own, boring into him. Glaring into the rainfilled twilight, he could almost imagine he did see her, a mocking smile on her lips as she warned, "The more you try to escape us, the tighter the net will draw, binding you to us, my poor Justin."

The old never-to-be-quelled resentments arose to prick him. "Hag," he cried, then brought a hand to his mouth, remembering where he was and with whom.

Hastily, he glanced about him and then he saw his unwanted companion and flushed. For a moment the past had intruded upon the present and he had actually forgotten her. With some concern he noted that she was lying very still and then he remembered concernedly that it was also her second fall that day. Crawling to her side, he put a hand to her heart. Much to his relief, he found that it was beating strongly. Either she had swooned or hit her head when they had been thrown from the coach. He ran a gentle hand through her hair, prodding for bumps, but found nothing. Seeing her cap lying a few feet away, he retrieved it and since it was sodden from the rain, he shoved it into his greatcoat pocket and then felt for the flask with which he had helped revive Nancy that afternoon. He did not find it. Evidently, he had forgotten to put it back. A faint groan alerted him and, bending over the girl again, he found her eyes open, blinking against the rain. Staring up at him, she frowned, "Why did you push me off?" she accused.

For a moment, he was too astounded to speak. "Push you off . . ." he managed finally. "I had nothing to do with that. 'Twas the man beside me . . . the other passenger, pushed the two of us down. I pray you are not in pain."

She regarded him a little suspiciously, quite as if, he thought angrily, she still doubted him. However, she said only, "I expect I ought to be in pain . . . but I have only a slight headache."

"Probably you hit your head when you fell," he explained.

"It's very wet . . ." she murmured.

"The rain," he acknowledged wryly. "My umbrella . . . is gone with my luggage . . . on the road to Preston."

"That person . . . you were very rude to him."

The faint note of accusation he heard in her voice served to infuriate him. "Miss Pemberton," he retorted icily, "whether I was or was not—rude to him—does not entitle him to try and murder us. It is a miracle we're not in worse straits. I think that, again—it was the rain that saved us—turning the earth to mud. If we'd fallen on the hard ground, we might not now be talking about it." He peered around him. "We must find some manner of shelter . . . there are trees growing at the edge of the road. "Can you move?" He reached out a slightly shaky arm, "Let me help you."

She shook her head, "I think I am able to move." She half rose and fell back. "Oh, my head . . . I am dizzy."

"Here . . . let me assist you." Rising, he was about to help her up when she managed to scramble to her feet.

"Where do you want me to go?" she asked.

"These trees should give us some shelter . . ." he indicated a small cluster of firs.

She eyed them dubiously, "not much. I wonder where we are?"

"I am not sure." He tensed as the sound of hooves reached him. For one wild moment, he wondered if the stage might have returned for them, but he quickly assured himself that such an occurrence was highly unlikely. Swinging around, he stared up the hill and into his field of vision rumbled a farm cart, its driver covered by a large tarpaulin. Hurrying into the middle of the road, Sir Justin waved frantically. Though the man gave no sign of having seen him, as soon as he reached the bottom of the hill, he drew rein, and lifting a corner of his streaming covering, he peered down at Sir Justin.

"Eh . . . eh . . . eh, wot's amiss, then?" he inquired in a broad Lancashire dialect.

"We . . . my . . . er, nephew and myself are the victims of foul play. We were pushed from the Preston stage as it came down this hill. We are much shaken up and we need shelter from the rain. Is there an inn nearby?"

"Can't say as there is," the man grunted. "Pushed off the stage were ye . . . 'tis not the first time I've 'eard o' that in these parts. Been 'appenin' frequently o' late. One man were kilt . . . 'twas fortunate you were not. 'Ow be the little lad?"

"Shaken . . . it was the mud that saved us."

"The mud'n the 'and o' God more like. Where be the youngun?"

"Here, sir," Livia, speaking in her piping treble again, stepped forward.

Sir Justin, who had felt a large throb in the region of his throat or his heart, he was not sure which, was reassured. In her masculine attire, her face spattered with mud and her short hair plastered against her head, there was nothing of the fashionable lady about Miss Pemberton. She looked like a young and scrubby lad. He put an arm around her shoulders and felt her move restively at the contact. However, keeping it firmly in place, he said, "As you can see . . . my nephew had a bad tumble."

With a click of his tongue and a shake of his head, the man said, "Aye, poor lad . . . Lord, Lord, 'e looks all done in . . . it's dryin' off ye'll need an' something 'ot to put in yer belly else ye'll catch yer death—the both of you."

"Could you perhaps put us up for the night? I can pay," Sir Justin reached for his purse and paled. It was gone. All at once the actions of the man who had fallen against him and then so violently pushed him from the stagecoach were explained. A professional thief, he had plied his trade to very good advantage and then neatly disposed of his victims.

Four

The curtains were billowing out the window. Turned into thin streamers by the wind, they grew longer, longer, longer until they stretched all the way down the street. Livia, watching this strange phenomenon, saw that they had been grabbed and held by Lord Ormond, who was staring up at her out of hard black eyes and well he might stare because she was only in her nightgown and Nancy was laughing immoderately. She slapped Nancy's cheek only to find that her hand was on Marianne's face—but Marianne continued to laugh because Livia was not wearing any clothes at all and her uncle was scolding her and . . .

"Miss Pemberton . . . Miss Pemberton . . ."

Responding to an insistent pressure on her shoulder, Livia awakened with no regrets. The dream had been terribly real while it had lasted. She opened her eyes to find the room filled with the gray-pink light of early morning. Immediately, upon moving, she was aware of stiffness in her arms and legs and of assorted aches and pains all over. Looking up, she stifled a gasp as she met the dark gaze of her dream which belonged not to Lord Ormond but to Sir Justin Warre. For a split second, she was shocked to find him there. Then, she remembered that he had shared the attic room with her, sleeping on the floor near the door, wrapped in one of the blankets from the bed. She also remembered that she had protested the arrangement only to have him reply sharply, "There's nothing else we can do. That farmer believes us to be uncle and nephew and I'd be loath to disabuse his mind of that."

"I was but thinking of your comfort," she had told him timidly.

"It's late for that," he had replied ungraciously, adding, "nor do I need mollycoddling."

Meeting his eyes now, she stifled a sigh. Despite his consideration, she was aware that he must be cordially hating her for her deception. Though he had not demanded any explanation the previous night, she knew that the time of reckoning was not far in the future.

"How are you feeling?" he demanded coldly.

"I am fine," she said, resisting an impulse to dwell at greater length upon her aches and pains. Though it could forestall the pending confrontation, she shrank from giving him the impression that she was a frail female. "Did you rest well?"

"Well enough," he returned curtly. "We must decide what we will do, Miss Pemberton." In a voice that was low but edged with a deep anger, he added, "Whatever prompted you to such folly?"

Livia ran a nervous hand through her hair and was momentarily stunned by the feel of her shorn locks, which she had hurriedly and inexpertly hacked off the previous afternoon. "I wanted to go ... to Gretna Green," she said in a small but defiant voice.

"And decided upon this ridiculous imposture. I had hardly thought that a young woman of your ... but I expect I should not be surprised. Such willfulness and irresponsible behavior seem to be a family characteristic."

Livia sat up, glaring at him furiously. "If you are suggesting that I am in any degree like Marianne ..." she began.

"I had not thought so ... but your actions ..."

"Predicated upon those of my uncle," she cut in. "I am well able to take care of myself. Yet, I am to sit back and wait while ... while ..." tears filled her eyes.

"I beg you will not give way to your emotions," he said icily.

She sniffed, "I am not ..." a thought struck her and she regarded him with wide, frightened eyes. "Oh, God, what are we to do?"

"Do you have any money?"

She flushed painfully and looked down, "Not more than a f-few shillings."

"'A few shillings,'" he repeated, his dark eyes fixed on hers. "You came upon this ... this venture with no more than a ... few shillings?"

Resentment rose and died in her breast, "I . . . gave most of what I had in my reticule to the postboy for his clothes and for his s-silence. I thought that you . . ."

"Would supply the rest?"

She swallowed. "Yes," she hung her head. "I was not thinking clearly. So m-much of my own p-plans went into my disguise." Her chin went up. "Also, I have never been allowed to . . . to carry much money with me, for all I am said to—to possess a fortune."

He exhaled a long breath and said in softer tones. "It is true, Miss Pemberton . . . if I'd not been robbed, I could have supplied all we needed. Unfortunately, I myself was not thinking clearly. If I had been, I should have known that villain for what he was. Certainly I have heard enough tales concerning what may befall travelers who are forced to ride outside or even inside our coaches . . . but be that as it may, I fear that, as they say in vulgar parlance, we are in the basket."

"But . . . what will we do?"

"We must first find out where we are. If we are closer to Wigan, we'll make our way back there. If it be Preston, it is possible that at the inn, I shall be able to explain our plight and dispatch a message to your uncle. We must take our chances."

"B-But if we have so little money," she faltered. "How shall we manage to—to travel?"

His expression had never been more sardonic. "Do not fret, Miss Pemberton. We shall employ a method used by our ancestors and still much in favor today. We shall go on foot."

● ● ●

The sun was high in the sky and though its brightness was occasionally dimmed by a drifting white cloud, more often it was not. The chill of the preceding day was gone and as Mr. Wilkinson, the obliging farmer who had sheltered them for the night, had obesrved, "Ye can expect 'twill be uncommon warm." It was uncommonly warm—warm enough to bake some of the soreness out of tired and assaulted limbs, warm enough for Sir Justin to remove greatcoat, jacket and waistcoat, carrying them over his shoulder along with Livia's—or rather the postboy's—greatcoat. She had protested this last service, saying she could carry it herself, only to be sharply reminded that however much she might look the part, she did not possess the endurance of the boy she was supposed to be. "We need to make time. It should not take overlong to walk eight miles, but since we are both unfamiliar with the lay of the land, it would be best that you did not tire yourself by assuming unnecessary burdens."

They were bound for Preston—a distance which Sir Justin had dismissed as short. Livia, who had dono some walking through the park at Riversedge, her estate in Sussex, could not agree. Nevertheless, motivated by pride and dislike, she had done her best to keep up with him. Now faced with a road which seemed to be entirely uphill and rocky besides, there was an unaccustomed and very uncomfortable pull at the backs of her legs and she was growing very weary. Perhaps a hundred yards ahead of them was a small copse. She longed to ask him if they might rest in the shade of its trees but, again, pride stilled her tongue. Such a request was bound to bring a frown and another sarcastic comment on the subject of feminine weakness. It would be one she could not refute—being all too aware that she was an unneeded thorn in his side or, perhaps his foot—since that would be even more painful. She was thinking a great deal about feet, her own being sore and badly blistered. The postboy's shoes, though small, were not small enough, and constantly rubbed against her heels. She longed to remove them and go barefoot, but the road, with its small jagged rocks and hard pebbles, would not be any the less uncomfortable, and for Sir Justin to find her without shoes might further assault his highly developed sense of propriety. She felt a stinging in her eyes. Tears were threatening. For once they did not arise from contemplating Lord Ormond's cruel deception and defection, but rather from an awareness of her own towering stupidity in assuming this ridiculous disguise! At the inn it had seemed to be her only alternative—yet, now she was in reluctant agreement with Sir Justin that it had been the very pinnacle of folly! Though, amazingly enough, he had refrained from telling her so, she knew that all their troubles stemmed from it. If she had not come on the stage with him, he would not have felt it his duty to prevent her possible falling off and, thus, he would have been alerted to the presence of the thief.

By now, he would have been in Preston or, more likely, on his way to Lancaster. By sunset, he could have been near Carlisle and by dawning in Gretna Green. As it was, they would need to return to Wigan and ... she shuddered, thinking of her uncle's biting lecture and Lady Maude's subsequent horror. Then, since servants could never be effectively muzzled, the story would leak out and be whispered in drawing rooms throughout London and in the country as well. She would be disgraced and the rest of her life must needs be spent in seclusion at Riversedge doing good works but never, no matter how old she grew, atoning for the fact that she had spent several unchaperoned days and nights in the company of a man! It would not matter in the least that she cordially disliked that same man and that he detested her!

"Miss Pemberton . . . Miss Pemberton . . ."

Livia looked up, startled to find that Sir Justin, having reached the top of the road, was some distance ahead of her. Wrapped in her thoughts she had done precisely what she had not wished to do—she had fallen far behind. As she hastened toward him, she girded her loins for a tongue-lashing, for he was frowning. Coming closer, she saw that he was also looking very warm. His face and hair were wet with perspiration. He had removed his cravat and his thin muslin shirt was plastered against his chest. Meeting his critical stare, she sighed. "I—I am sorry t-that I fell b-behind. I—I was t-thinking," she said lamely, despising herself for stuttering and hating him the more for making her feel so guilty.

He said coldly, "And no doubt you are unused to such exercise?"

She would have given much to be able to contradict him but, unfortunately, that was impossible. Her life in London this past season had been largely sedentary. Other than walks or rides in the park with Lord Ormond, her main occupation had been in having fittings for her trousseau and for her bridal gown; she winced at the memory and in answer to his observation, she said, "It was a cold winter. I was much indoors."

"Should you care to rest?" he demanded.

It seemed to an indignant Livia that he had never sounded more sarcastic or more contemptuous. "No," she drew herself up. "I am not in the least tired."

He inclined his head, "How fortunate for you, Miss Pemberton. I wish I might say the same, but it seems I lack your endurance. I *am* tired." There was a gleam of sardonic amusement in his eyes. "I should very much like to sit by that stream I hear splashing in the woods yonder. Perhaps you would not mind sharing a little of the bread and cheese our host was kind enough to provide for us."

"Bread . . . cheese . . ." she repeated. It occurred to her that she was not only hungry, she was ravenous. However, sternly quelling the enthusiastic response that threatened to burst forth from her, she said with an elaborate shrug, "If *you* feel in need of refreshment, I should not mind."

"I must admit that I do," he returned. "And I must thank you for being so accommodating, Miss Pemberton."

Something stirred in Livia and against her will, her lips twitched into a smile which, to her great annoyance, was the prelude to a laugh which, again, she could not repress. It seemed to be catching, for he, too, laughed.

"Come, then, Miss Pemberton, for even if neither of us is fatigued—we must need rest if only because we must remember that we sustained two hard falls yesterday and neither of us being ... indestructible, it behooves us to husband our strength." Moving to the side of the road, he cautioned, "Best follow where I walk and watch out for holes. The hare, the hedgehog and the badger are active hereabouts."

Livia, obeying and relieved he did not expect her to match his stride, felt some of her prejudice dropping away. He had seemed kinder and more human. If she still could not like him, at least, she did not actively hate him.

A half hour later, she was still of the same mind. Though he had said little, he had not looked upon her with that disdain which had been so apparent the previous day. They had eaten some of the bread and cheese—not all, for she had agreed with him that there was no telling when they might arrive in Preston. As he returned their provisions to the sack, she sat gazing at the stream which ran over mossy stones and some hundred yards distant followed a dip in the ground, turning into a waterfall and ending in a small pool. This last was visible from where she was sitting, through a gap in the surrounding trees, and ringed with ferns and willows, she found it a pretty, even a beguiling sight. She wished she might wade in it or, better yet, immerse herself completely in those cool waters and wash away the grime of the road. She felt very sticky and worse yet, dirty. She was also positive that her nose had turned an unbecoming red which might easily be the condition of her whole face—for the sun was hot. Sir Justin's naturally swarthy complexion seemed even darker. She wondered a little at his coloring—certainly his deep brown, nearly black, eyes and blue-black hair were un-English. No doubt he had some French or Italian ancestry.

"Miss Pemberton . . ."

She looked up quickly. There had been an edge of impatience to his tone. "Had you been speaking to me before?"

He nodded. "You were lost in a reverie. Are you yet tired?"

"Oh, no," she was quick to assure him. "I feel most refreshed."

"Really?" Again there was a gleam of amusement in his eyes. "And here I was thinking I should like to stretch out and sleep a little before we get under way again. The sun is at its zenith and perhaps it were better if we waited a bit before we return to the road. However, if that is not agreeable with you . . ."

"Oh, it is," she cried. "Most agreeable." Seeing one corner of his mouth twitching into a smile, she added sharply, "though if you are humoring me, I assure you . . ."

"On the contrary, I am humoring myself. *I* am not ashamed to admit that I am tired."

Livia lifted her chin. "*If* I were tired, I would not be ashamed to admit it, either."

His smile broadened. "So be it, Miss Pemberton." Moving closer into the shade of a tree, he stretched out and closed his eyes. Somewhat to her surprise, he fell asleep immediately.

Though she was minded to follow his example, the splashing of the waterfall was once more loud in her ears. On an impulse, she moved away, walking along the bank and edging around the trees. In a few moments, she had reached the pool. It was even more beautiful and more inviting than it had appeared from where she had been sitting.

Mirror-clear, it reflected the ferns, the surrounding trees, the bright blue sky and her own image—this last sight bringing forth a gasp and a moan of dismay from her. Though Livia had never been vain about her looks—at least not as vain as her cousin Marianne—she did not believe Lord Ormond had lied when he had told her that her eyes were singularly expressive and beautiful. Nor had she been in total dissent with his description of her pale but luminous skin. And, on one occasion, when he had extolled the smoothness of her hair, telling her that the style, done by Nancy to resemble one she had found in *La Belle Assemble*, gave her a resemblance to a Raphael Madonna, she had admitted her agreement by instructing Nancy to continue dressing it that way.

Sinking down on her knees, she mournfully eyed the face that stared back at her from those pellucid and all-too-revealing depths. Her first thought was that dear Roderick would never have known her; her second was that it was not in the least surprising that Mr. Wilkinson had believed Sir Justin's explanation concerning his "nephew" and her third thought was that no one, not her best friend nor her worst enemy (Marianne) would have recognized this ill-kempt, grimy, sunburned urchin with the shock of jaggedly cut, wildly curling hair as the quietly elegant young lady known as Miss Livia Pemberton.

Tears rolled down her cheeks, leaving in their wake white streaks which gave further proof of just how grimy she had become. It also brought to mind her earlier wish to cleanse herself in that same pool and the wish being father to the thought, she glanced toward the barricade of trees, hoping that she might glimpse Sir Justin and see if he were still asleep. Reassured by the sight of his recumbent form, she stepped behind a willow tree and, stripping off her garments, she folded them neatly, put them a safe distance from the bank, and dove into the pool. When she came to the surface, it was with her mouth firmly sealed against a threatening scream. Though she had gone swimming in a Scottish loch which lay on the estate of a friend of her aunt's and found it very cold, though she had also swum in the sea at Brighton, she had never imagined anything could be quite as cold as the water she now found herself in. For a second, she had the impression that she had leaped into recently melted ice but in a very few moments the chill passed and if she did not feel precisely warm, she was not so cold that she could not enjoy swimming back and forth across the pool. It was wonderfully refreshing and exhilarating. Furthermore, she was ridding herself of dirt and grime. Looking into the water, she received some small satisfaction from her reflection. If her face remained pink with sunburn, at least it was clean and if her hair was plastered down and dripping, it would soon dry out as soft and as fluffy as it was when washed by Nancy.

Nancy. It was amazing how far away that life seemed. Yet less than a week earlier, Livia Pemberton had been wont to awaken in a soft, comfortable bed, prop herself up against lacy pillows and sip her morning chocolate, prior to having the bath brought in and Nancy to dress her and braid her long hair. She winced. Her present situation would have been unthinkable, horrifying to that other Miss Livia Pemberton. If that young woman had been able to gaze into a crystal ball and see herself garbed in boys' attire and trudging down a dusty country road in the company of a hard, bitter man with whom she had nothing in common save a mutual misfortune— both of them having proved wanting by those upon whom they had fixed their affections, that Livia Pemberton would have dismissed her startling vision as a bad dream. It was bad—and yet, despite the frowning presence of Sir Justin, despite the eventual and inevitable ostracism that must be her portion once he had brought her back to her uncle, she was, she realized with a shock, not as miserable as she ought to have been. It was wonderfully pleasant to swim in the pool and she had also found it amazingly comfortable to wear the postboy's breeches and shirt. She had never realized how very confining her gowns and her Circassian corset had been. She laughed and was startled by her laughter. Three days earlier, she was quite sure that she would never be able to smile—much less laugh— again. She tensed. It seemed to her that she had heard an answering laugh, low and unpleasant.

She looked around her but saw nothing. Had it been her imagination? She continued to listen but all she heard was the sound of the wind through the trees—or was it the wind? Out of the corner of her eye, she saw the lower branches on one of the trees close to the water's edge quivering, quivering far more than it would under the assault of a mere breeze. She stared into the pool and then froze with horror, for, in addition to her own face, she glimpsed another, half obscured by the leaves of the tree. It was a man's face, bearded and ugly, but it was his eyes that shocked her the most—they were small, beady and their expression chilled her to the bone. With a cry of fright, she dived down, down, down into the depths of the pool, but she could not remain in that watery fastness—she could only hold her breath a few seconds! She hurriedly swam toward the bank farthest away from that tree and emerged among the ferns in time to see the branches quivering again and to hear another low chuckle, even more unpleasant than the last. She half raised herself, trying to see through the trees. If she might awaken Sir Justin...but she could see nothing from her present position. As she moved away, she heard a plop and a crackle of the underbrush as if the man had leaped from his perch.

"Wot's the matter little lady? Didn't mean to startle ye, but yer a sight I never expected to see, a regular mermaid, eh?" His voice was as horrid as his appearance. He came to stand at the edge of the pool, a husky man in ragged trousers and with a filthy shirt hanging open displaying a chest covered with grayish-black hair, growing nearly to his chin. "Come out...I want to see ye again...all of ye." He was shaking with laughter. "Thought ye were a lad until I seen ye peel."

She shuddered. All the time she had thought herself alone, that lout had been watching her. "Go away," she tried to say, but no sound would come forth from her fear-constricted throat.

"Come out, lovely...I won't 'urt ye. Wouldn't

want to 'urt ye . . ." His insinuating speech grated on her ears—he was walking around to the spot where she was clinging. She pushed herself away from the bank.

"If ye won't come out, maybe I'll come in'n join ye . . ."

Seeing him step closer to the edge of the pool, Livia found her voice and screamed loudly.

"No use yer yellin' little lady. 'Tain't no one to 'ear ye'n no use to be scared. Like I said . . . I wouldn't 'urt ye . . . not me."

"Sir Justin, help, helppppp meeeeeeee," she shrilled frantically, praying that he was awake—but he had been sleeping so soundly!

"Where are you?" she heard a deep voice call from some distance away. Thank goodness! He was awake!

"H-Here . . ." she screamed with all her might. "The p-pool . . . downstream the w-waterfall."

He burst through the trees faster than she would have imagined and, hurrying down to the edge of the pool, he stared at her confusedly. "What's amiss . . . did you fall into the water?"

Since, for a moment, it looked as if he might leap to her rescue, she held up a white arm, motioning him back, "I . . . I did not fall," she cried. "But there's a man . . . a p-person who . . ." even as she spoke, she heard a crackling in the bushes and guessed that her tormenter was fleeing.

Turning in the direction of the sound, Sir Justin corroborated her suspicions. "He's going . . ."

Livia, aware that he might be able to see far too much of her, swam quickly back to the sheltering ferns. "T-Thank you," she quavered. "I w-will g-get out now."

"I shall wait here until you do."

"You cannot . . . I . . . I am . . . I d-do not think he—he will be back." She was feeling very cold again. "I must get out," she continued plaintively.

"Indeed you must," he agreed. "I shall wait by the trees. I shall not look, I assure you." He spoke with an indifference which, for some reason she could not fathom, angered her, but he had come to her rescue and she had no right to be angered at anything he might think or say or do. She swam to the willow tree and hoisting herself up on the bank, cast a scared look over her shoulder. She did not see Sir Justin. Quickly, she slipped shirt and breeches over her dripping body; it was most uncomfortable but there was no help for that. Shoving her feet into the shoes, she winced as her lacerated heels came in contact with the leather, but again there was no help for that, either. Feeling much in the wrong, she came to find him still standing near the pool, staring up at the sky.

"I am ready," she murmured, hardly daring to look at him.

"Good. Let us be on our way." he responded curtly.

Turning his back on her, he strode back through the trees, Livia following in the distance. Suddenly he stopped. Peering about wildly, he whirled to face her. He was shaking his fist and his face was distorted by fury.

"W-What is it?" she quavered.

"Our garments . . . our food, everything, gone."

" 'Gone'?" she repeated blankly. "Gone where?"

"'Where'?" he yelled. "Stolen, damn you. Do you not know that these woods are filled with vagabonds? But why do I ask . . . you who went swimming in that pool . . . you who . . . there is no end to your stupidity! I knew that directly I laid eyes on that fortune hunter you were ready to wed."

Fury thrilled through Livia. Oblivious of their present predicament, she cried, "He is not a fortune hunter. He is rich in his own right. He . . ."

"Balderdash. He is up to his eyebrows in debt. I have that on very good authority!"

"The authority of my uncle, no doubt. He is wrong. I tell you that he has a fine estate and . . . and . . . but why do I trouble to defend him. You are determined to believe the very worst of him!"

"And you are not. Interesting."

"I know Marianne," she retorted. "She is utterly ruthless and my uncle was forcing her to . . . to . . ." she broke off, oddly reluctant to hurt him any more than he had been hurt already but on meeting his blazing eyes, she knew it was already too late.

"Forcing her to marry *me*, is that it? Is that what she told you?"

"But surely you knew . . ."

"I know only that the poor child is an utter romantic, who had her head turned by an unscrupulous beggar brought into her ken by your own folly in not reading his character more accurately. If you had had any common sense, he would never have been able to cause her pain. You say she was being forced to marry me. Perhaps that is the construction you choose to put on it, but it was not true. She . . . we were very happy until . . ."

Livia drew herself up. "Sir Justin, if you believe

that, then I must tell you that I am not the only one wanting in common sense!" she retorted grandly. Turning away, she started to move up toward the road but stopped confusedly, realizing that however much she despised him, she dared not go on without him.

His harsh laughter filled her ears as coming to her side, he demanded, "And where might you be bound, my girl? Into the arms of that creature who surprised you at your ablutions?"

She knew herself to be blushing all over her body. "You insufferable ... oh, God." Facing him, she saw his thin muslin shirt, all he had to wear against the chill of an April night. In a low, trembling voice, she said, "S-Sir Justin, I am sorry about your l-loss of garments. It was all my fault. If I hadn't cried out ... I am so sorry for all the trouble I have caused you."

"And so you should be," he returned ungraciously, "but for you I should have reached Gretna Green on the morrow ... and would have had some opportunity of talking sense to Marianne and now ..." his own gaze softened, "but forgive me. I fear I am forgetting that you, too, have suffered. Come, Miss Pemberton, let us be on our way while the sun's still with us. The milk's long spilt and soaked into the ground. Our tears and lamentations will not bring it back. It's very possible that both of us should have realized that in the beginning."

"Yes, I ... I fear that's true. It may have been madness to ... to pursue them," she admitted ruefully.

"Aye, madness," he said heavily, "but let us

rectify our mistakes by finding some sensible way out of his imbroglio." Determinedly, he started back toward the highway and, resignedly, Livia followed him.

Five

The sun was lower on the horizon and a cool breeze was blowing. Livia guessed that it must be a little past three. They had covered several miles; it felt like a thousand on her raw and bleeding heels but Sir Justin had told her it was no more than five. His conciliatory mood had vanished and she could guess that he was worried for more reasons than one. In the last two hours, two post chaises and three farm carts had passed them and though he had tried to flag them down, he had only been liberally coated with dust as they had vanished in the distance. Livia did not hesitate to ascribe this lack of success to their appearance. A man in a sweat-stained shirt, breeches that were beginning to look the worse for wear and boots that would have been the better for polish—walking with a poorly clad youth did not inspire confidence—and what would be their reception at the inn? If either of them were to avow that they possessed the monies to buy such a place, lock, stock and barrel—she could imagine they would be driven forth as lunatics!

"Please . . . walk faster," Sir Justin urged.

Livia expelled a short annoyed breath. Her habit of thinking had put her behind again. "I am sorry, I shall hurry," she answered apologetically. She had not mentioned the blisters. It would only remind him of how much she had already impeded his progress. Perhaps if she were to take longer strides, it would serve her better. It felt a little awkward at first, but even if she could not equal Sir Justin's steady pace, it did appear as if she were covering more ground. Unfortunately, just as she was getting used to this form of locomotion, her foot caught in a root and sent her sprawling. Before she could right herself, he had turned around.

"Oh, Lord," he said resignedly, "did you hurt yourself?"

Stung by that long-suffering tone, Livia replied loftily, "Not in the least." Springing to her feet, she faced him defiantly. "See . . . I only tripped." She stepped forward and stopped with a sigh. She had lost one of her shoes.

"Here . . ." he had sighted it by the side of the road and kneeling to pick it up, he was about to hand it to her when, with an exclamation of horror, he caught sight of her blistered foot. "Good God, Miss Pemberton, what is this?" he demanded.

Livia shrugged elaborately, "The shoe's a bit too large for me. It's nothing, I assure you."

"Let me see your other foot," he commanded.

"It is well enough."

Unheeding, he slipped off that shoe noting with horror the rough sores. "Why did you say nothing?" he demanded fiercely.

"I have told you, they do not hurt."

"Liar! It must be agony to walk on them. Indeed, it's a marvel you've been able to walk so far."

"I've not complained."

"Am I expected to commend you for your bravery? Well, I shall not. Lord, Lord, how have you lived twenty-three years in this world and . . ."

"'Twenty-three years'!" she was momentarily diverted. "I've not lived twenty-three years in this world, Sir Justin. I became twenty-one in November. Last November."

"Indeed, well, twenty-one or twenty-three, you should know better."

"It could not have been my uncle told you I was twenty-three," she mused. "It must have been my cousin."

"It little matters," he said brusquely. "What does matter is that you could get dirt in these sores and if they were to become infected . . ."

"I expect that she told Roderick that I was twenty-three also," Livia said indignantly.

He glared at her, "Will you stop nattering on about that? You may have turned twenty-one, but for all the common sense you've displayed, you might be twelve or even a little under." Reaching into his pocket, he brought forth a length of muslin, which she recognized as his discarded cravat. Ripping it in two, he quickly bound each of her feet.

Then, before she quite knew what he was about, he had scooped her up in his arms.

"Put me down this instant!" she commanded angrily.

"Place your arms around my neck. That way you'll distribute some of your weight and, please, Miss Pemberton, do not wriggle."

She continued to wriggle. "Put me down!" she repeated furiously. "You cannot carry me. I am far too heavy."

"On the contrary, you are amazingly light. I expect that in common with many other foolish females, you starve yourself so that you might appear a veritable sylph."

"I do nothing of the kind. F-Furthermore, you've no right to . . . to t-treat me as if I were a—f-fool, when I . . ." to her chagrin, Livia found herself close to tears.

"Miss Pemberton," he said crisply. "If any of your actions had ever given me cause to believe that you were not a fool, I might be more forebearing, but as it is, I am guided in my estimations of you by your own conduct—or the lack of it. Now—let me explain that we must endeavor to reach our destination before eventide. In my present state of undress, I might easily come down with an ague—if forced to brave the night air overlong. I am well able to carry you—far better than you are able to walk with those badly lacerated heels. Now . . . for both our sakes, I pray you'll treat me to no more of these absurd cavils."

Thus summarily rebuked, Livia found herself with words literally crowding onto her tongue and ready to be spewed forth in a fiery response. Yet, in her present situation—not to mention location—discretion, she decided reluctantly, was by far the better part of valor. Furthermore, she found that, as he strode along, he did seem largely unencumbered by her weight. Though he was not as tall as Lord Ormond, not much above average height, she would not be surprised if he were the stronger of the two. His arms were powerfully muscled and his chest broad. Too, there was no denying that she was much more comfortable than she had been while struggling after him on the ground. If he were angry, if he disliked her, if he found her presence an almost intolerable burden, it did not carry over into the way he was holding her—there was a gentleness in his grasp that surprised her.

They had gone a little more than half a mile when she heard the sound of wheels behind them. Setting her down carefully, Sir Justin turned, then frowned, as a gaily painted caravan drawn by a pair of sturdy horses came into view. "Gypsies!" he exclaimed disgustedly. "We can look for no help from those rogues."

However, as the caravan neared them, it was possible to see that its driver bore no resemblance to a gypsy. He was a fair young man with a shock of pale yellow hair. His wide blue eyes were set in a broad face which, while not unprepossessing, bore signs of having suffered considerable punishment. His nose had been broken, and more than once by the look of it, his right cheek was badly scarred, and his smile revealed that one of his front teeth was missing. However, it was a pleasant smile and evidently reassured by his appearance, Sir Justin wavered.

Livia was relieved to see the caravan drawn to a stop as its driver cocked an interrogative eye at them. "Will ye be wantin' a ride, then?" he asked in a soft mild voice much at variance with his battered physiognomy.

"Yes, my nephew's sore of foot and if you are going as far as Preston, we'd be much in your debt if you could take us up," Sir Justin explained.

"I be goin' a bit o' the way toward Preston, but I turn off at the forest—for 'tis to Lancaster I'm bound—to the fair, but I'll be glad to 'elp you out." The man fastened an intense gaze on Livia, who looked back at him nervously, fearing that he might have penetrated her disguise. But he only shook his head and gave her a commiserating look. "Your feet is it? Not used to the road, eh, my lad?"

"No, he's not. I was bringing Oliver here—from his school. He thought it would be a fine adventure to ride outside . . . but as it turned out, we were robbed and thrown from the Preston stage. The poor lad was badly bruised, I fear," Sir Justin explained with a glibness Livia found astonishing.

"Poor little tyke," the man shook his head. "I've 'eard as 'ow there's been more'n a bit o' trouble on the Preston run . . . folk takin' to ride it for just such a purpose." He gave Sir Justin a penetrating stare. "You talk like one o' the Quality."

Livia saw Sir Justin stiffen. "Would you expect one of the . . . er, Quality to be riding on the stage?" he inquired lightly.

"I dunno as to that . . . the man wot I left a ways back . . . 'E talked like you." His expression turned downcast. "I dunno wot I'm to do wi'out 'im. 'E were in 'is cups most o' the time, 'tis true, but come a bout'n 'e'd sober up long enough to talk for me. 'E could talk grand. 'E knew just wot to say. Dunno 'ow I'll find another 'ereabouts."

" 'Talk' . . . talk about what?" Sir Justin inquired.

"Me. You see I be on a sparrin' tour . . . bein' as I'm a pugilist. Name's Roarin' Bill Pickett . . . may'ap you 'eard o' me? They say as 'ow I'm a comin' man."

"I do not believe that I have," Sir Justin told him. "But I know very little about . . . er . . . mills."

" 'E were the same," Mr. Pickett nodded. "But the things wot 'e said about me . . . they was wonderful. I 'ave me a book . . ." He jerked his thumb toward the caravan. "Tells about some o' the Pets o' the Fancy . . . Cribb 'n Jackson . . . Ye must o' 'eard o' Gentleman Jackson, sir?"

"Yes, I have heard of him," Sir Justin nodded. "Cribb and Molyneux, too."

Mr. Pickett's eyes gleamed. "I seen Molyneux fight . . . 'e were good in 'is day. 'Twas some as thought 'e were the devil, 'im bein' so black'n all. 'E were a devil in the ring . . . couldn't nobody stand up against 'im at first. 'Ad 'im a good manager, too. That 'elps. 'Elps to 'ave someone in your corner. Arthur . . . that's the man wot traveled wi' me until 'e began to see things comin' at 'im . . . 'orrible things—dragons'n such . . . went outa 'is ead, you know. The Blue Ruin . . . but afore 'e went crazy, 'e usta read the book'n 'e'd get off afore a mill'n talk about 'ow I were stronger'n Molyneux . . . talked about some cove name o' 'Ercules wot was the strongest man o' 'is time. I can't tell you all 'e said but it were beautiful . . . made 'em look up sharp . . .

97

them wot wanted to challenge me . . . I wish I could remember all 'e said, but I'm not good wi' the gab. Only wi' my fives, see?" He held up a huge hand and folded it over into a fist. "You talk like 'im," he looked wistfully at Sir Justin. "You wouldn't think o' comin' wi' me to Lancaster, Penrith'n Carlisle . . . wouldn't take more'n a week . . . I'd pay good if you could talk for me. Wouldn't make no mind if you 'aven't never done it. 'E 'adn't either . . . but 'e read the book'n made up some on 'is own . . ."

"You say you'd pay?" Sir Justin asked.

"Aye, I paid 'im . . . I gi' 'im three pound a town'n 'is board'n lodgin' to boot. 'E spent it all on the Blue Ruin. Did 'im in, like I said. You don't look as if you're partial to it."

"I am not," Sir Justin told him with some distaste.

Listening to them, Livia held her breath, hoping that what she guessed might be Sir Justin's strongly developed sense of pride would not keep him from accepting an offer which, while it might delay their return to Wigan, could also solve their current and extremely pressing problem of food and lodging.

She wished she dared persuade him to accept the offer. Then, it occurred to her that in her character of "Oliver," it might be highly unnatural if she did not try. "Oh, Uncle," she said eagerly. "I've never been to a mill and I've always wanted to go. The other boys at school, they've all told me how exciting it is. I'd also like to go to the fair."

Mr. Pickett grinned, "The little lad'd find it mightily to 'is taste, 'e would."

Sir Justin regarded Livia quizzically, "'Twould end all hope of reaching either of our destinations and I cannot think that a fairgrounds is the proper atmosphere for a . . . my nephew."

"Eh, I do like to 'ear you talk . . . yer even better'n 'e, were'n your nephew wouldn't take any 'arm, not wi' me about." Mr. Pickett crooked his arm, revealing a biceps of almost alarming proportions.

"Uncle," Livia raised her eyes to lock glances with Sir Justin, "have we any choice—with night coming on and all? As for our destinations, I'll not repine if our plans are changed. And you need not return to your position until the end of summer." In an aside to Mr. Pickett, she explained, "My uncle's a tutor to a wealthy family in the south."

"Oh, that be grand. I always wanted an eddication. I c'n read a bit but I go slow-like. Wouldn't ye come? I'll pay good like I said—four pound—even five'n yer own tent. You could stay in the caravan wi' me, but 'e always wanted it that way'n I expect you will, too."

"Uncle, it would be the better way." Livia urged.

"Well . . ." Sir Justin spoke slowly, "I think you might be right, nephew. It would be a solution. I cannot say as to whether or not I can 'talk' with all the fluency of your friend Arthur but I expect I can try."

Livia, giving him a relieved and approving look, clapped her hands, "Oh, Uncle Justin, I am so glad."

She received a darkling stare, "You needn't

99

imagine you'll be allowed to run wild over the fair-grounds. It's no place for . . . for a lad of your tender years."

"I'm sure 'e'll be good as gold," Mr. Pickett averred.

"Oh, I shall, Uncle Justin, I truly shall."

"Justin . . . I like that name. Wot else're ye called, sir," Mr. Pickett inquired.

". . . Strong," Sir Justin answered after the barest hesitation.

" 'Strong,' eh?" The pugilist startled them by bursting into laughter so loud that the reason behind his sobriquet of "Roaring" Bill was self-evident. "That be good that be," he said when he could summon enough breath to speak again. "You be strong'n so be I. An' see if we don't both do just fine."

"It's a marvel, I've not taken to the Blue Ruin myself. Indeed, I think I must be suffering from its effects even without a draught of it," Sir Justin remarked as he stood back looking at a small tent he had just erected beside Bill Pickett's caravan.

Both were under a tree in a section of a vast meadow dotted with booths and tents, stables and stalls. Though the preparations for the fair were largely completed, there was still some activity in their area. A banner advertising a miraculous juggler had just been unfurled and two men were busily tacking up a vivid depiction of a muscular gentleman in a lion skin. The lowing of cattle being prodded into pens and the baaing of sheep resounded through the grounds. Occasionally wildly barking dogs would rush excitedly around the premises only to be driven off with sticks, stones and curses. Groups of curious little boys with a penchant for touching, peeking and even taking were being ruthlessly hustled out by rough-looking persons with grim expressions on their battered faces.

Livia, who had been watching Sir Justin's exertions with some interest, shrugged elaborately when she met his accusing gaze. Though she could well understand the compunctions that had occasioned his plaint, she was far from sharing them. She was much too intrigued by her surroundings. They had arrived at the fair site early that morning after a night spent in Bowland Forest—more specifically in the caravan, which she had found to be surprisingly commodious. In addition to a built-in table and chairs, a minute kitchen, and shelves for provisions and for Mr. Pickett's belongings, there was room for a large bed and also for a smaller folding cot which the pugilist proffered to Sir Justin. However, Livia had slept on the cot, Sir Justin having explained to a surprised Mr. Pickett that his nephew needed the rest, having only just recovered from a bout of measles. As on the previous night, he had lain on the floor. Despite her surroundings, despite the loud snoring issuing from Mr. Pickett's corner, Livia had gone to sleep as easily as ever she had in her whole life. Upon awakening, she had found herself marvelously refreshed.

Now, it was well into the afternoon and she was amazed that having risen with the birds and endured several more miles of a bumpy ride in the interior of the caravan, she did not feel in need of the nap that Miss Livia Pemberton had been in the habit of taking every day—but, again, she did not feel like Miss Livia Pemberton, not in the least. It was as though, upon assuming the identity of Sir Justin's nephew, she had literally become the boy Oliver. However, judging from his chance remarks, it was obvious that the man who had decided to call himself her uncle had not made so easy an adjustment. She could well imagine that it warred with his highly developed sense of propriety to see her standing in her boys' clothes, barelegged, her injured feet thrust into open sandals of his own fashioning ("after a Roman design," he had explained when he had given them to her). Out of monies advanced by Mr. Prickett, he had provided her with a new pair of breeches and a cotton shirt for which she was most grateful, since they were a much more comfortable fit than the postboy's togs. He had also made purchases of his own—buying black corduroy breeches, high leather boots, a blue and white striped shirt, a bright red velveteen waistcoat and a spotted neckerchief.

"If I am to be a barker for a pugilist, I must look the part," he had said somewhat defensively on meeting her appraising and slightly amused glance.

Though she had not commented, she could not help thinking that his new garments were extremely becoming to him, far more so than the conservative apparel he had donned for the journey from London. She was pleased that he had not smeared pomade on his hair—much preferring to see his dark locks fall into their natural heavy waves. With a jolt of surprise, she realized that he was actually a very handsome man. She wondered why she had never noticed that before and realized that heretofore she had always compared him, much to his detriment, with Lord Ormond. A second surprise was in store for her—on thinking of Roderick, she had not experienced the pain his name usually engendered. She was also aware that she had not really thought of him for the whole of the morning. Of course that was missing. No wonder, for he, too, had had much else to occupy her mind. She hoped that Sir Justin had also experienced a similar surcease from his own woes.

Scanning his face, it seemed to her that he had. The brooding look, so apparent two days earlier, was missing. No wonder, for he, too, had had much to occupy his mind—namely, their highly compromising situation, which, if were ever to be revealed ... she sobered suddenly. If such a thing were to happen—there would certainly be unpleasant and far-reaching consequences. Inwardly, she quailed. If, by some terrible mischance, her family were to learn about these shared intimacies, it was quite possible that Sir Justin might be forced to marry her. That would be dreadful indeed—for both of them. However, she reflected quickly, there was little likelihood of her uncle or aunt ever finding out about the exigencies with which they had contended. Now that they stood to receive money, they could concoct some manner of tale that would satisfy all concerned. What that might be, she did not know, but there would be time enough to think about it. Meanwhile, it behooved her to try and persuade Sir Justin to consider her as "Oliver" rather than as that foolish young woman who had upset all his plans. That last thought made her unhappy—she wondered if he were still hating her for having kept him from pursuing Marianne—but, again, she could not think of that, either. It was the present that must needs occupy them. She said lightly, "Uncle Justin, you promised me we could go to the castle once you'd set up the tent."

He wiped a hand across his perspiring brow, "Is that all you can say?"

"I expect it's what I should say were I..." she cast a quick glance about her and though there was no one within earshot, she lowered her voice, "Oliver."

"And were I your tutor uncle," he muttered, "I should have known better than to bring a child your age into this highly questionable atmosphere. Have you any notion of what it will be like on the morrow —with thousands of people crowding into this meadow? And 'twill be even worse where I am... God knows what manner of brute will offer to floor our champion. You are not to come near there... Lord, Lord, I cannot think what made me agree to this preposterous scheme!"

"Lack of funds," she said promptly.

"True but..."

"And," she interrupted, "I had best remain at hand during Mr. Pickett's bouts."

"No."

"Yes... else he will think it very odd. Measles, my dear uncle, wild horses, too, would not keep Oliver away from a mill. I must be there."

"No."

"Yes."

"No, I say!"

"Yes, if you're wise."

"By heaven..." he looked at her curiously. "I vow I do not know what to make of you... a gently bred female like yourself, a blue . . ." he broke off, looking self-conscious.

"Ruin . . . or stocking?" she inquired. Before she could reply, she continued speculatively, "I cannot think that you meant to say 'ruin,' so it must have been 'stocking.' A bluestocking, a distinction conferred upon me by Marianne, no doubt? There seems to be no end to her generosity—what with granting me two extra years of existence and . . ."

"Miss . . ."

"Shhhhh," she put a finger to her lips. *"Oliver* . . . Oliver at all times and at all cost."

An unwilling smile tugged at the corners of his mouth, "Oliver, then."

"Thank you, Uncle Justin. Now—as I define it, a bluestocking is a female who dabbles in literature. I read literature but I do not write it. Consequently, I must deny Marianne's allegations as relayed by yourself."

"I do not consider it in the light of an 'allegation' . . . or as I expect you are terming it—an 'insult.' I . . ." he began.

"Ah, but you are prejudiced, sir. And . . ."

"Miss . . . er, Oliver, if you would be kind enough to allow me to finish what I was about to say. I do not scorn females who write books. Indeed, I find them far more to my taste than those whose heads are filled with such deep considerations as what gown they will wear to the Prince's ball but . . ." he broke off, his frowning gaze fixed on a spot beyond her.

Looking in that same direction, Livia saw several caravans coming to a stop at the far end of the meadow. Older and dirtier than that owned by Mr.

Pickett, they were driven by dark, swarthy men garbed in old clothing and battered hats. As she watched, a group of small, equally swarthy children tumbled out, followed by women in brightly colored gowns. Even at this distance she could see gold coins glinting about their necks and dangling from their ears. "Oh, the gypsies are here!" she cried.

"Yes," he replied curtly. "Come to prey on the gullible and bilk the unwary. No fairgrounds is free from them."

"I like them," she said. "They used to camp on our estate when I was small . . . I found them very interesting, too."

"Many a poor woman has, to her sorrow," he replied. "You must not exhibit the same interest here. They have sharp eyes and can spot that which others might not see."

"Oh, then may I not have my palm read?"

"Most assuredly not! Stay clear of them. They can bring you nothing but trouble. They are fleas . . . lice . . . parasites, who burrow deep into our English soil, yet sow no seed and reap no harvests save trouble. Do you propose to stand there gawking at them or should you like me to take you to the castle?"

For a moment, Miss Livia Pemberton was highly offended by his mode of address. Then, seeing a deep anger in his eyes, she had a feeling that it must have arisen out of some unhappy experience he had had with one of the Romany tribe. She said pacifically. "I should very much like you to take me to the castle, Uncle Justin."

She was rewarded by a wry grin. "Come, then, boy," he said, and strode off across the meadow.

● ● ●

The hill crowned by the castle stood less than a half-mile away. From below, the castle had seemed small, too small to house the prison which yet lay behind its thick walls. However, on coming up to one of its terraces, which was as far as any visitor might go, Livia thought it was the town that looked small, a place of gray stone cottages and narrow winding streets. which badly needed the bright splashes of color to be found in the neighboring meadow. Turning away, her eyes widened and she expelled a long breath.

"You are winded," Sir Justin said. "I fear we walked up here too quickly. Your insistence on being a lad has mesmerized me into being careless."

"I am not winded . . . I am breathless," she contradicted, turning to gaze with delight at the distance that was Morecambe Bay—blue and shining with gulls diving over it and sailing ships upon it. She glanced once more at the old castle. "It was John of Gaunt who built that gateway and who said 'this precious stone set in the silver sea . . .' That sea's not silver . . . but it's very beautiful."

"It was Shakespeare who put those words in Gaunt's mouth," Sir Justin remarked.

"Dwelling here, he might have thought them."

"As might have those who lived here before that castle was built. 'Civis Romanus sum.'"

"I am a Roman citizen," she translated. "But, of course, they were here long before. I know it was a Roman camp . . . castra, Lancastrum built on the River Luna."

He looked at her in some surprise, "And you'd

not the time nor the funds to purchase a guidebook, I'm thinking."

"It was not necessary." she smiled at him. "Oliver excels in Latin and finds his history fascinating. He hopes that when he is a man, he'll be able to follow that old wall of Hadrian through the sheep pastures and sometime see a helmeted and shielded shadow on the grass and know he has glimpsed the shade of a centurion set to guard it through eternity." She added with a self-conscious little laugh, "I pray you'll not think your nephew too fanciful."

"No," his voice was muted. "I cannot scold him for a fancy that I have entertained, myself."

"Oh, yes, I do remember. Marianne told me that you shared my uncle's interest in the ancient Romans."

"Since a child ... I'd guess there were many Roman stones embedded in the foundations of this castle. I know that it's true of the ruin that rises on our lands."

"Where are your lands?" she asked.

"In Hampshire ... not far from Portchester Castle ..."

"Where Henry V assembled his men before sailing off to fight at Agincourt."

"You do know your history."

"Yes, as I have explained, I do love to read. Are your lands near the sea?"

"One can see it from the battlements of Warre ... that's the name of our home."

"Battlements ... it is a castle, too?"

"There's a Norman keep remaining ... the rest of the house was rebuilt in the last century by my grandfather. It was he who put up the battlements.

I fear he was much influenced by Horace Walpole. They were cronies until...he wed and retired to Warre."

"Then...Warre is a Gothic structure...with secret passages and such?"

"All the excesses of the style," he said contemptuously. "My grandfather was a true Romantic. He revered the writings of Rousseau. In common with him, he rebeled against the established order, exalting the primitive wherever he could find it. He could quote whole chapters of *La Nouvelle Héloïse* and did so to my grandmother, who, I fear, did not appreciate them as much as he thought she must."

He had spoken with a bitterness so intense that Livia felt chilled as well as confused. It was obvious that he resented, perhaps even hated the man. "Did you know him?" she asked diffidently.

"He died when my father was scarce breeched."

"And your grandmother?"

"She survived," he said shortly.

"Was she also a Romantic?"

"Fortunately, she was practical. Very. I am much in her debt. Though my grandfather was loath to credit her with it, she had an excellent business sense and what she did not understand she found people whom she trusted to explain. Consequently, the ancestral acres yet remain in the hands of the Warres—or Warre, I should say, since I am the last of them—when there were many who thought they'd be lost and hoped they might be."

" 'Hoped'?"

"Where there's land, there's hope and scheming relatives. My grandfather had no business sense at all. His affairs were badly tangled when he died.

However, to the surprise of all concerned, it was discovered that he'd wed a female who knew how to hold her own against the vultures."

All at once, the reason for the bitterness with which he had described his grandfather became clear to her. Despite its Gothic excesses, he must love his home—his lands, as well. He could not have cherished very pleasant memories about the man who had nearly lost them. She would have liked to know more about his youth, which, it seemed to her, might have been unhappy, but feeling she had questioned him enough, she contented herself with saying, "I am glad of that. And there's a Roman ruin upon your lands? Part of a castle?"

"Part of a villa . . . a very small part. A few bricks carefully embedded in mortar . . ."

"The old walls of Portchester Castle are still standing, are they not?"

"They are . . . and there are relics to be found in its vicinity. As a boy, I used to elude my tutors and go hunting for them."

"Oh," she breathed. "Did you find any?"

"Some coins and a small glass vial made to harbor tears."

"Oh, I've seen those in the British Museum," she said eagerly. "When I . . . when Oliver was younger, he longed to have such adventures but his leading strings were, I fear, far more binding than yours."

"Did he chafe much at that bondage?"

"I am not sure that he did. He was mainly concerned with the restraints upon the mind—typified in his own mind by a favorite and oft-quoted aphorism of his governess, 'A little wit is of value in a woman much as we value a few words spoken plain by a parrot.'"

"And did that governess actually believe that this statement must be taken literally?"

"She said that it was the better part of wisdom in a female to behave as if she possessed none. I rebeled against that dictum, wanting to be valued for more than my—portion."

"So I have been told," he said with the trace of a smile.

"By Marianne?"

"By Marianne, who mentioned something of the nature of your discourses with gentlemen but did not explain the reasons for the catechism."

"I am sure she did mention that she believed me slightly mad."

"I do not think she understood you. She's very young, after all."

"The gap between eighteen and twenty-one's but three years."

His eyes lingered on her face, "I begin to believe it's not a gap but a chasm lies between you and your cousin. I cannot imagine that you've ever been very content with the lot of being a female—at least in our society."

"That's not entirely true. You must not go by my disguise, which I admit to have been ill-considered. I was not discontented with being a woman. I wanted only to find one with whom I might share a communion of the spirit and the mind as well as . . ." she shrugged.

"And you thought you'd found him in Lord Ormond?" he asked incredulously.

She was momentarily indignant. "He did not

talk nonsense to me. He is extremely well read. And he even composed a poem for me. I thought... but..." she sighed.

"A poem? *He?*"

"*He!*" she flared.

"I can scarce believe it."

"Shall I give it to you?"

"Please."

"It's not very long."

"I should not expect that it would be."

"It goes thus:

> Dark hair has a warm appeal,
> Gray eyes that speak of zeal
> And the light that glows within
> Stems from a soul that knows no sin
> Livia, Livia at thy altar let me be
> For thou art worthy of my idolatry.

"You see?" she said with a certain melancholy satisfaction.

"I see that I have wronged him. Most certainly, I undervalued his intelligence. If one is going to steal, let it be from an obscure poet."

"'Steal'?"

"Steal, yes. What you've quoted's the work of Sir Guy St. Leger."

"I've never heard of him!"

"Few have. He was a minor—a very minor Cavalier poet. It is only by the merest chance that I am acquainted with his verses. We have an extensive library at Warre and in my youth I was an omnivorous reader. Consequently, I came upon St. Leger's poems—published at his own expense in a volume so thin, he would have been better advised to have inscribed the whole upon a broadsheet. If you'll substitute the color blue for gray and the name of Julia for Livia, you'll have the whole of it. It was said that it was dedicated to that same Julia whose 'liquefaction" of silken clothing so pleased Robert Herrick. Unlike Herrick, Sir Guy was killed defending his king at Preston, I believe, thus putting a period to his versifying—not much of a loss to English letters, I fear."

"Oh," Livia murmured.

"I am sorry if I have caused you pain, Miss Pemberton."

"My pain," she replied in a small voice—"should lie in my own error."

"You could not be expected to recognize . . ."

"Not the verse, perhaps, but now that I think of it, there was much else that he said which did not ring true. His conversation was often stilted, as yours never is." An unwilling laugh escaped her. "I begin to think that you may be right concerning his interest in my fortune. Under those circumstances, think of the pain I have caused him."

"Pain . . . *you?*"

"I can imagine him burning many a candle as he delved into Greek drama. Undoubtedly, some one of my rejected suitors must have told him what to read. Oh, dear, oh, dear . . . I begin to think I had a most fortunate escape and poor Marianne . . ." she came to an abrupt stop, seeing a frown in his eyes. "I am sorry . . . I keep forgetting that you . . . that she . . ."

He broke in harshly, "No matter." Turning away from her, he stared down the path that led back to the fairgrounds. "I think we'd best be going.

Pickett will be wondering at our absence. Come, Miss Pemberton."

"Oliver," she prompted.

"Oliver, then," he rasped. Reaching out a hand, he added, "Let me help you. The way is steep."

She eluded his hand. "I need no help. It's all downhill."

"As you choose."

Quickly. he went down the steps from the terrace. As Livia followed close behind him, she was angry at herself for forgetting that the wound inflicted by Marianne must yet be painful, doubly painful to a man of his pride. He would not be as quick to recover from her cousin's cruelty as she, Livia, from that of Lord Ormond. She halted.

Until that moment, she had not realized that she had recovered—at least not so completely. She still could not be entirely sure. Closing her eyes, she conjured up an image of her faithless bridegroom and found it to be blurred—not unlike a watercolor that had been left in the rain. With a lift of her spirits, she realized that she was, indeed, free of him. She hoped that Sir Justin would soon be similarly released from his wasteful and hurtful passion. He did not deserve to suffer needlessly. She was surprised again. She had, she realized, undergone yet another reversal of feeling. She no longer disliked or resented Sir Justin. On the contrary, there was much to admire about the man.

Since he could not change the situation into which he had been catapulted—partially by her own folly—he had obviously determined to make the best of it. This demonstrated a forebearance of which she had not believed him capable. Therefore it was incumbent upon her not to get into any more scrapes . . . she had already tried his patience far too . . . she frowned. Her thoughts were becoming strangely convoluted. She was confused by them. It was unlike her to . . .

"Miss Pemberton!"

Startled, she looked around, realizing that his voice was reaching her from some distance away. Then, she saw that he was standing at the bottom of the hill. Hurriedly, she ran down to join him and, in accordance with her half-formed resolutions, she listened meekly to his adjurations concerning the dangers attendant upon becoming separated from each other in this unfamiliar territory.

When he had concluded, she said solemnly, "Yes, Uncle Justin, I assure you that it will not happen again." She was relieved to discern a gleam of amusement in his eyes.

"See that it does not, my boy," he commanded in his guise of stern relative. "I cannot always be about to watch over you."

"I understand that," she replied and was conscious of a strange throbbing in her throat. Shock nearly brought her to another standstill. However, mindful of his injunctions, she managed to keep moving, albeit considerably more slowly than before —as she considered the nature of that most unwelcome sensation. She had had similar feelings in the days when she had erroneously imagined herself in love with Lord Ormond. Certainly, she had not expected to experience them again. Having done so, she was forced to a new and horrid conclusion. It was altogether possible that her release from her late passion might be predicated upon a feeling for

Sir Justin Warre that far exceeded mere liking. It was a daunting thought. In addition to making her wonder if she had taken leave of her few remaining senses, she was all too cognizant of its utter futility. Even if Sir Justin were to fall out of love with Marianne—which seemed unlikely, she could not imagine that he could cherish anything approaching tender passion for the unprepossessing little waif that she had become!

Six

Having reached that most startling conclusion concerning the new state of her heart, Miss Livia Pemberton, following close behind Sir Justin as they approached the fairgrounds, was doing her best to banish it. Yet, as she watched him striding purposefully forward, she found herself unable to keep from admiring the proud set of his head, the breadth of his shoulders and the slimness of his waist. She could even be pleased that he had not attained the great height of Lord Ormond. It had always given her a slight crick in the neck to look up at him. However, it was not Sir Justin's appearance that had excited her admiration, at least—not entirely. It was his mind and his ready acceptance of her own intelligence. If she had only met him in London during one of her three miserable seasons. She wondered why he had never appeared in London. Presumably because he did not care for the frivolous and idle life of the ton. She remembered her uncle praising his plan of retracing the steps of the ancient Romans. Her eyes narrowed. It was not entirely impossible that Lord Semple, impressed as much by Sir Justin's fortune as by his archeological proclivities, had deliberately encouraged him to remain away from the city and the snares set by parents with ambitions similar to his own.

It was a cruel trick, she thought resentfully, to foist the nubile Marianne upon him. Her uncle was not unaware of his daughter's failings—he knew full well that she was no wife for a man of Sir Justin's intellectual attainments. However, if Marianne were not intelligent, she was shrewd, and judging from the morsels of information Sir Justin had dropped, she had not, despite her piteous complaints to Livia, been unkind. Livia let out a long hissing breath. It was more than likely that Marianne had beguiled her time in the country by practicing her wiles upon him. Her anger increased as she remembered her cousin's chatter concerning the taking of a lover and blithely cuckolding this man. She shook her head in bewilderment. She had never had any respect for the girl's judgment—but she had not believed her daft! How could she have failed to perceive his true worth? How could she have preferred Lord Ormond's bovine good looks to Sir Justin's striking presence? Still, she, Livia, could only be thankful for her cousin's singular lack of discernment. If it had not been for that—Marianne would now be Lady Warre, while she would be wed to Ormond and, no doubt, they would be having uncomfortable and pointed discussions about money. The idea of such a union brought a curl of distaste to her lip. If the truth were to be told, she was much obliged to the young woman who must now be calling herself Lady Ormond.

"Good God in heaven!" Sir Justin exclaimed, halting so quickly that Livia nearly bumped into him.

"What's amiss?" she demanded in some alarm.

"Look there," he muttered, gesturing at a couple just across the road near the entrance to the fairgrounds.

Following his pointing finger, Livia experienced a similar jolt of surprise as she saw a young man, a farmer by his dress, with a length of rope in his hand. Its other end was knotted loosely around the waist to a most beautiful girl. She was clad in a much laundered blue cotton gown which served to outline every curve of a magnificently proportioned shape. Her face was oval and her features would not have looked out of place on a classical statue. Her hair, a ripe gold in color, rippled in unfettered waves down her back and her feet were bare. Despite the rope, she held her head high, and her eyes, a deep violet in hue, were filled with an expression of scornful defiance. It was evident that she must have heard Sir Justin's involuntary exclamation, for she had come to a stop and was regarding him curiously.

"'Ere . . . move along wi' ye," ordered her captor crossly, with a surly glance at Sir Justin.

"I'll take me own time," she replied.

"Ha, ye'll need to soften yer answers for 'im

wot'll buy ye . . . on the morrow. Wot ye need's a strap to yer back. An' I'm in 'opes ye'll get yer just deserts. 'Tisn't every 'usband'll be as kind'n forebearin' wi' ye as I've been."

"'Kind' . . . 'forebearin',' the 'ell ye were," she cried.

"What does he mean . . . 'buy' her?" Livia whispered.

"It's an old country custom," Sir Justin muttered. "I'm surprised you're not acquainted with it. As a child I saw a butcher auction off his wife. The bids stopped at a little over a pound—but he took that with a pint of ale thrown in."

"But that's terrible."

"It's not unusual amongst this class."

"She's so beautiful!"

"Beauty is as beauty does," Sir Justin's lips curled back in a mirthless smile. "You and I should have learned that lesson well."

A day . . . an hour earlier, Livia would have hastened to agree with him, but now, at this evidence of his lasting bitterness and aching heart, she could only feel depressed. However, she managed a sigh, "Yes, I expect we have."

"Come," he whispered. "Let's see what price he's put on his Venus."

As he strode toward them, Livia felt a sharp little pang, which she had no trouble in recognizing as jealousy. It was evident that he was attracted by fair-haired women. Her burgeoning sympathy for beauty-in-distress dwindled alarmingly, as she saw the girl give Sir Justin an appraising stare that held more than a hint of cajolery.

120

"You're selling your wife?" he asked the farmer.

"Aye," the man growled. Looking at him more closely, Livia was surprised at his appearance. He was not ill-dressed or ill-looking. Furthermore, he had a frank open face and a mild expression that contrasted very oddly with his rough speech and surly manner. "Should ye be wantin' to buy my Bessie?"

"Not I, my friend. But I should be surprised if you had much trouble in finding a customer."

"D'ye think so?" Bessie smiled at Sir Justin. "I 'opes yer right."

"Do you *want* to be sold?" Livia could not help blurting.

"Aye," she nodded. "'Tweren't wot I liked bein' wed to Joe 'ere." She shot her husband a resentful look.

"Wot gets she'll 'ave the worst o' the bargain," her husband snapped. "'Er thinks as she's too good to work on a farm." Grabbing one of her hands, he held it up, "Look ye . . . lily white."

Pulling her hand from his clutch, Bessie rolled her eyes at Sir Justin. "I got my . . . uses," she drawled.

"Not to me, you 'aven't. I need a wife'll 'elp me in the fields as well as . . . elsewhere, not a great lazy slut 'oo lies abed till noon'n don't lift 'er 'and to nothink." He looked at Sir Justin. "Ye c'n 'ave 'er cheap, man. Three pound'n she be yours."

Sir Justin laughed, "I fear not. I am not in the market for a lass."

"I wouldn't mind workin' if I were wed to 'im,"

121

Bessie smiled. "I like the way 'e talks. You ain't from around 'ere, are ye?"

"Wot's it to you?" Joe demanded.

She actually flashed him a smile, "I want to know."

"My nephew and I are from London," Sir Justin told her.

"Lunnon, is it," Bessie's eyes gleamed. "I 'ave always wanted to go to Lunnon but Joe 'ere ..." she broke off suddenly at a glare from her husband, adding a split second later, "May'ap 'im wot buys me'll take me to Lunnon'll dress me up fancy-like in a yeller silk gown'n buy me an 'at wot's got cock feathers atop it."

"Ha," scoffed Joe, "more likely 'e'll take a switch to yer rump." Joe fixed his eyes on Sir Justin. "Wot ye be doin' so far from Lunnon. Come 'ere for the fair?"

"We came with Roaring Bill Pickett ... I'm his barker."

"Roarin' Bill," Joe exclaimed. "Is 'e 'ere ... last time we seen 'im ... 'e were at Nottingham ... be good to meet 'im again ... 'andy pair o' fives 'e 'as, eh, Bessie?" he grinned.

"Aye, may'ap ye can sell me to Bill," she replied pointedly.

"Nah, 'e's got more sense'n that, but I'm glad 'e's 'ere." His grin suddenly vanished. "C'mon, it's time we went some place where they'll want ye. An' tomorrow, I might 'ave enough o' the ready to lay a bet on Bill." He jerked at the rope.

"Ow," the girl shrilled angrily, "that were too 'ard by 'alf, damn ye."

"More o' that talk'n ye'll get the back o' me 'and," he retorted ferociously. Glancing at Sir Justin, he added. "May'ap, I'll be seein' ye tomorrow'n I'll stand ye to a pint." Without waiting for an answer, he jerked at the rope again and strode off at a fast clip that brought him more loud but unheeded complaints as his wife stumbled after him.

Livia shuddered, "What a dreadful man. That poor girl, can no one help her?"

Much to her indignation, Sir Justin broke into a merry laugh. "Yes, a thorough-going rogue, I'll agree." Putting an arm lightly over her shoulders, he continued, "Come, nephew, it's time we were picking up our feet else Bill will think we've bolted."

Activated by his touch, a flurry of odd pulses went through her and for once she was glad of her sunburned skin, for surely it must not reveal the flush that was heating her cheeks. In that moment, she wished Bill's caravan were a thousand leagues distant. Unfortunately, the banner, emblazoned with a highly idealized depiction of Mr. Pickett in the throes of throttling a hapless opponent, was no more than a hundred yards distant. However, in spite of this new and utterly delightful sensation, she still felt it incumbent upon her to say, "Surely, you cannot countenance a man selling his wife."

"No, certainly I cannot, but in this instance . . ." he broke off and Livia was startled by the sudden presence alongside them of two dark young men, who had evidently been headed in the same direction as themselves. One of them was hurling a stream of incomprehensible words in Sir Justin's direction.

Dropping his arm and turning away from Livia, Sir Justin said coldly, "If you are addressing me, I am afraid I do not understand you."

Apparently undaunted by his forbidding attitude, the man spoke to him again in the same language. It was an odd tongue, Livia thought—it sounded foreign, but there were English words mixed with it.

"I have said that I do not understand you," Sir Justin retorted icily.

"Aye, pal, you understand," the other insisted, smiling boldly, even insolently into his eyes. "You understand with the Shuro and the Kan . . ." Laughing loudly, he moved back to his friend and linking arms with him, muttered something that caused them both to laugh uproariously. Then, with a final impudent glance in Sir Justin's direction, they moved toward a garishly painted caravan that stood near a tent on which displayed a large yellow palm with astrological symbols done in black on each of its red lines. As they neared it, a small woman emerged. She was wearing a bright orange gown, and golden earrings swung from amidst her black locks. She smiled at the two men. Then, at a word from one of them, she, too, glanced in the direction of Sir Justin and waved.

"More gypsies . . . and she must be the fortune-teller." Livia said.

"Aye, and you will keep away from her," Sir Justin frown. "Damn cheating . . ."

"Why don't you like them?"

"How might one like them? As I told you—they are parasites . . ." There was fury in his eyes but there was anguish, too. "I expect you wonder why

124

they spoke to me? My grandmother was a Spanish woman, dark-complected as I am and the gypsies ... some of them, persist in mistaking me for one of their cursed tribe."

"How very odd ... when it's easy to see that you're nothing like them," she said gently.

His eyes rested on her face and she read suspicion in their black depths as he replied brusquely, "Yes. it's damned odd and it's been damned embarrassing as well. I know that some of our poets find them fit subjects for wild romances, but they know little of their ways. But we've idled long enough." Moving away from her, he walked off swiftly, vanishing among the booths.

She followed slowly, wondering if this was something else her uncle had known and, because of his cupidity, overlooked. He must know it, she decided, and wondered why she, who had seen so many gypsies as a child, had not guessed that some of their wild blood ran in the veins of Sir Justin Warre.

Something had awakened Livia. Lying on the heap of cushions that Sir Justin had made into a bed for her, she stared into the darkness—aware of words spoken loudly but, at present, all she heard was the sound of Sir Justin's even breathing. As usual, he lay near the entrance. She was glad that he had not been aroused by whoever must have passed the tent. He needed his sleep. Undoubtedly, the morrow would hold new and possibly trying experiences for him. Hopefully, they would serve to take his mind from the incident of the afternoon. Though he had not mentioned it again, she knew it must be weighing on him, for he had turned very quiet and there had been a sombre, brooding expression in his eyes.

She had yearned to comfort him but she had not dared. If he were to even suspect that she doubted his careful explanation, she was uncomfortably positive that it would destroy the tenuous bond between them. She had a feeling that there were deep-seated reasons for his resentment toward his gypsy kindred. Thinking on it, she realized, too, that he had made an oblique reference to that heritage in his bitter description of his grandfather's passion for Rousseau. Undoubtedly, the man had married a Romany woman, and the "vultures" he had mentioned must have been those relatives who had deplored the misalliance and sought to have the child disinherited. It must have been very hard for her grandson to have grown up among people who hated and distrusted the gypsies. Memories were long in the country. She could recall having been shown a pond in the village adjacent to Riversedge. It was there that one Sukey Cleaver, having been betrayed by the local blacksmith, had drowned herself. Her nurse had spoken as if the tragedy had taken place the day before yesterday—actually, it had occurred in 1719. It could not have been more than fifty or sixty years since Sir Justin's grandfather had taken unto himself his gypsy bride. She could imagine the slurs that must also have been the lot of her grandson. It was possible that he had known rejection all of his life. It would account for his absence from town and also for his choice of avocation. Her thoughts drifted toward Marianne and she winced.

Under those circumstances, the trick she had played upon him was doubly cruel.

She tensed. The sound that had originally awakened her was in her ears again. "*Jasa tu chovihani ... Jasa ... Jasa ...*"

Startled, Livia realized that it sounded like the language used by the young men who had accosted Sir Justin that afternoon. This time, she had no trouble in locating the source. It was he who had cried out, was still crying, "Begone, witch ... why will you haunt me?"

In the dim moonlight that squeezed between the tent flaps, Livia saw that he was sitting up, "Leave me ... *Jasa ... Jasa ...*" he continued to cry.

She hurried to his side, "Justin ... Justin ..." putting her arm around his shoulders, she shook him gently.

He awakened instantly. "Is anything wrong?" he demanded.

She was suddenly aware that his shoulders were bare. She removed her arm hastily, saying "You called out ... you must have been dreaming."

"I called out ... what did I say?" he asked edgily.

"I don't know. It was mostly gibberish, but it seemed that you wanted someone to go away. I am sorry I awakened you."

"It was as well you did," he said gravely. "It was a bad dream and one I am the better without. Best go back to bed, my dear. I wish I'd not disturbed you."

"No matter, I shall fall asleep very quickly, I am sure."

127

Moments later, huddled among her cushions, Livia felt foolish, yet, at the same time, strangely happy because he had addressed her as "my dear." Unfortunately, common sense, reasserting itself, told her sternly that such a term meant nothing to him. She meant nothing to him. She was only a burden to him and because of her unfortunate relationship to Marianne, she was also an unwelcome reminder of her cousin's perfidy. Tears coursed down her cheeks. Her hands still tingled from contact with his smooth skin and if she had entertained any doubts on the matter, they had vanished. She loved him. In fact, she wished herself beside him, cradling his dark head on her breast and telling him that she should not mind were he *all* gypsy!

Turning over, she buried her hot face in the pillows. She was well aware that such fantasies should never have entered the head of a well-bred, respectable and unmarried female. It was no comfort at all to realize that since the moment when she had come forth from St. Martin-in-the-Fields, none of her actions had been those of a well-bred, respectable and unmarried female. Something very strange had happened to Miss Livia Pemberton. It was extremely disconcerting. Even more disconcerting was her realization that she only regretted it could not go on happening for the rest of her life!

The fair, the fair, the fair! Under a bright blue May sky, it tentacled across the meadows like a gigantic octopus. Livia, awakening early and with some qualms stemming from her untoward ruminations of the previous night, had been feeling vaguely depressed but it was impossible to remain in that condition when confronted by the monstrous reality of the fair!

Seemingly, it had grown to immense proportions overnight. The crowds were so heavily numbered that they spilled over into the town itself, pushing, laughing, quarreling, gawking, breaking out into brawls and hair-pulling matches. By a little past one, the noise was deafening. Screaming mothers in search of lost children, screaming children in search of lost mothers mingled their voices with those of tray-bearing hawkers crying such wares as banners, flags, ribbons, badges, dolls, balls, monkeys-on-a-stick and pinwheels. Then there were scissors grinders, fat oily men proclaiming the efficacy of patent cure-alls, furious victims protesting the expertise of slithering pickpockets, barkers inviting the populace to witness the pig-faced woman, the Indian-rubber man, the handless painter, the footless dancer, the Chinese magician, the Arabian fire-eater and the Hungarian sword-swallower. Rope dancers performed on high wires and acrobats bounded below. Jugglers tossed balls and the ubiquitous Judy screamed epithets at Punch from the puppet theater. Frantic howls resounded through the air from riders braving the bumpy and creaking Up-and-Down or the whirling Roundabout, while neighs and snorts, baas and moos arose from the auctioning pens. The practiced whine of the professional beggars also added their quota to the din— and then there were the smells—acrid animal odors, the perfume of cut flowers, of plants, of vegetables, the smell of frying foods, of woodsmoke, of gunpowder.

To think of the fair as a whole was to be confused and intimidated. It needed to be narrowed down into sections, to the stalls of glass, china, pottery and wool which drew interested housewives, to bins of vegetables and counters covered with fresh-caught fish and slabs of meat, somnolent lobsters and barrels of clams, where cooks from neighboring estates haggled over choice portions. Children lingered by the sellers of candied apples, spun sugar cones, lollipops and peppermint sticks. Girls beseeched their lovers to buy them bright glass necklaces and brass earbobs, shell brooches, fans, ribbons and "gold" rings. There would also be china figurines—puppies, dolls, pipe-holders—and silver cups given as prizes in shooting matches, running contests, in smock-races and for merely knocking down a pyramid of bottles.

In the company of Sir Justin, Livia, who had been sadly bored by the newly opened Soho Bazaar of London and intimidated by its surging crowds, found herself as eager to view the sights about her as the boy she was supposed to be. Strolling from stall to stall, holding fast to his hand as sternly instructed, she had felt herself infected by the excitement around her. Yet once she was back in their section of the fair among the magicians, the fortune-tellers, the menagerie and the freaks, she found herself depressed. It was odd, for there was even more excitement to come. She was to witness Bill in action as he accepted the challenges of youths anxious to floor the champion, Sir Justin having agreed that this privilege must surely be accorded a boy of his nephew's age. He had not viewed the idea with any great show of enthusiasm.

"You'll not find it to your liking," he had warned. "There'll be blood spilled."

"I'd not be put off by the spilling of a little claret," she had answered in her best Oliver voice.

He had laughed but he had still seemed doubtful, "It's to be hoped you'll not swoon, for I shan't be able to dose you with brandy or hartshorn."

"Nor shall I require it," she had replied firmly.

His look had remained doubtful and while she longed to prove him wrong, second thoughts were coming to the surface of her mind. Would he prefer it—if she did faint? Did he admire the clinging rather than the self-reliant female? A vision of Marianne stole into her consciousness. She entertained it with resignation. Once more it was necessary to remind herself that it was Marianne he preferred, Marianne he had loved, might still love, and while he had been holding her hand as they had wandered over the fairgrounds, she was sure he had not thrilled to its touch. She was equally sure that when they had been hemmed in by the crowd at the Punch-and-Judy show, he had not experienced any excitement at being pressed close against her—so close he might have felt her heart beat even as she was aware of that same motion in his chest.

Sighing, she looked over her shoulder into the semidarkness of the caravan where Sir Justin sat talking to Bill. His new clothes became him, and earlier in the day she had noticed that his melancholy had largely vanished—engulfed, perhaps, by the excitement that surged around them. He looked younger and a little happier. Catching her eye, he smiled. A thrill coursed through her. As smiles went,

131

it was the best yet, being warm and involving his eyes as well as his mouth. However, on turning away, she caught sight of her feet, dirty from her walk and that reminded her of what he saw each time he looked at her. If only she had not donned her ridiculous disguise; but if she had not resorted to such extreme measures, she would be back at the inn with her uncle while Sir Justin would be in Gretna Green either reclaiming his lost Marianne or dueling with her husband—and she, Livia, would be bemoaning the loss of Lord Ormond and might never have come to love Sir Justin, which, under the circumstances, would have been just as well . . .

"Hssssst."

Startled by a whisper, which seemed just under her ear, Livia looked around but saw no one. Then, she was alerted by a scrabbling sound, and glancing down, she saw a panting, bedraggled young woman crouched low and crawling around the side of the caravan. Lifting a tearstained face, she cast a terrified look behind her and gasped, "They be after me . . . 'Elp me. Do."

With a shock, Livia recognized Bessie, the wife who was to be auctioned off to the highest bidder. Without stopping to question her, she jumped off the steps. "Go inside," she muttered.

As Bessie fled into the caravan, Livia, hurrying after her, pulled the door shut, and sitting down on the top step, she leaned casually against it. A moment later, two heavyset young men stumped in from the same direction as the harried girl. They, too, were panting and staring about them angrily. From their appearance, it was obvious that they were brothers. Both were bronzed and stocky, both

132

had the same small mean blue eyes, short sandy hair and blunt unprepossessing features. They halted near the steps, frowning. Beyond the caravan was the squared-off platform called "the ring" and across from it was the tent which Sir Justin had set up and into which one of the brothers peered. Livia noted uncomfortably that if Bessie had not dashed into the caravan, she would now be easily visible as she made her way around the ring.

"You seen a girl come past?" one of the brothers demanded.

"No, I didn't see nobody," Livia said wonderingly.

The two men looked at each other, "Where be she?" one of them demanded. "Seen 'er come this way."

"Gotta be in there," the other man pointed at the caravan. "Ain't no other place she could 'ide, Bert."

"Nah," the man called Bert nodded, and looking up at Livia, he added, "You been sittin' there all this while?"

"Nowhere else," she replied cheekily.

"An' didn't see nobody run past ye, lad . . . a girl?"

"No."

"Yer lyin'," Bert said menacingly. "We seen 'er come around 'ere, me'n Tom. We was right be'hind 'er." He edged closer to the steps. "Don't 'ee play any tricks, lad or 'twill be the worse for 'ee."

Her heart was beating faster, but she looked at them calmly. "I don't know wot yer talkin' about," she said in her clear boyish tones. "Who is it you want?"

Tom growled, "There be a lass wot be our'n. Bought'n paid for."

Livia opened her eyes wide, "A servant?"

"Not a servant," muttered Bert, "she . . ." a flush reddened his countenance, "don't matter wot she be . . ."

"She's in there," Tom jerked a thumb at the caravan. "'Tweren't nowhere else she could be'n we're goin' to take 'er outa there." He placed a foot on the steps and, reaching forward, planted an immense hand on Livia's shoulder, his fingers, hard as steel prongs, biting into her flesh.

Fear and outrage moved her to cry out more shrilly than she had intended, "Lemme gooooo!"

Hard on her cry, the caravan door was pulled open and Bill Pickett emerged, his formidable body filling the aperture. "Wot be the trouble, lad?" he demanded. Then facing the pair, he added, "Who be ye?"

At the sight of Roarin' Bill, Livia's assailant fell back, exchanging a look with his brother. "We be tryin' to find a lass," he explained.

"She come this way," Bert added, his belligerence manifesting itself once more. "Gi' us the slip, she did'n after us paid four pound for 'er."

"Four pound for a lass," Bill's glance was puzzled. He slowly scratched his head. "They be sellin' females at this 'ere fair?" With a glint of eagerness in his blue eyes, he continued, "Where be that stall. I be bound to it myself soon's I'm done 'ere."

The brothers glowered. "'Tweren't like that," Tom explained. "'Twas a man wi' 'is wife for sale. Bert paid two pound for 'er'n I paid two."

"Ye were goin' to share 'er like King Solomon?"

134

Bill asked with a slow grin. "Cut 'er down the middle?"

"No," Bert returned sharply. "Tom didn't 'ave the whole price'n I 'elped 'im . . . 'tis Tom wot bought she'n then she up'n give us the slip. Come this way, she did—wi' us 'ard be'ind she . . ." He gave Bill a penetrating stare. "She didn't come into your wagon?"

"Didn't see no woman," Bill shook his head.

"Don't know 'ow she could've got outa 'ere so quick," Bert muttered. "Maybe you didn't notice 'er comin' in, eh?"

Bill's eyes narrowed, "You suggestin' I'm a liar?" he asked.

Tom punched his brother's arm, "C'mon Bert."

"I tell ye . . ." Bert began, glaring at Bill and at Livia, "they be 'idin' the wench." He glared up at the fighter. "We'll find 'er though. She can't 'ide forever'n we'll be around when she shows . . . see if we ain't."

"I trust ye'll not be 'angin' around 'ere, friend," the pugilist spoke softly but his tone sent a thrill of fear through Livia. Obviously it had a similar effect on the brothers, for they seemed to tense simultaneously.

"We only want wot's our'n," Bert muttered, but when Tom punched him on the arm a second time, he followed him around the platform, vanishing among the tents.

"Oh," Livia breathed. "They were dreadful."

"I'ope they didn't 'arm ye, lad," Bill said.

"No," instinctively she touched her shoulder. "You came out just in time. What happened . . . I don't understand?"

"S-Shut the door," Bessie quavered from inside. "'Urry."

"Come in here, Oliver," Sir Justin called.

"Aye," Bill ducked back into the caravan, and Livia, following him, drew the door after her, closing it with a little bang as she saw Bessie huddled in Sir Justin's lap, her head pillowed against his chest.

Bill moved to her, "I seen 'em. Ugly pair o' brutes. Wot did Joe 'ave in mind sellin' ye to 'em."

Bessie raised her tearful eyes, "Couldn't do naught else. They offered four pound'n if 'e'd refused—everyone'd known it were a trick. I 'ad a terrible time gettin' away from em'n if they should see Joe . . ." she shuddered. "They was both 'orrible . . . the way they looked at me . . . a-diggin' at each other's ribs'n sayin' wot they was goin' to do once we was 'ome." She burst into tears again.

Her outburst had given Livia the information she needed and whether it was the sight of her golden hair spilling over Sir Justin's arm or the sight of his soothing hand upon her quivering shoulder, she felt a marked lack of sympathy for the woman. "You've done this before, I expect?" she questioned.

"Aye, they 'ave'n I been tellin' 'em 'twere a chancy lay'n bound to bring 'em more trouble'n they could rightly 'andle." Bill said solemnly, nodding his head several times in emphasis.

Bessie sat up, "Twas to be our last time," she sobbed. 'Twere for the little one wot's comin' end o' December."

Livia's incipient jealously was swiftly replaced by pity and concern. "They might be back," she warned. "What are you going to do?"

Bessie shook her head, regarding her dolefully.

Her bold airs of the previous day were gone. Evidently, she had been entirely demoralized by her experience. "I got to find Joe," she whispered.

"Where was you goin' to meet?" Bill inquired.

"Special spot . . . near the castle," she explained. "But 'ow'm I goin' to get to 'im wi' them lurkin' about? I shouldn't know which way was safe."

" 'Tis me'll need to bring you up there. You stay 'ere in the caravan till I'm through'n . . ."

"No," Bessie wrung her hands. "Joe, 'e were already wary o' them, too. Like I said 'e didn't want to leave me wi' 'em. If I don't show soon, 'e'll be comin' after me . . . 'E ain't strong enough to deal wi' 'em."

The pugilist looked at her doubtfully. "Don't 'ave more'n a 'alf hour afore the bouts . . ."

"Perhaps I could help," Sir Justin cut in.

Livia opened her mouth and closed it on a protest, fearing she might injure his pride. Yet, how she longed to warn him of bulging muscles, brute strength and fury, a formidable combination, especially when multiplied by two!

Fortunately, Bill was in unconscious agreement with her. " 'Twouldn't do for you to tangle wi' 'em."

Sir Justin nodded. "I was not suggesting it. I was thinking of the crowds. I could talk to them . . . pending your return."

Bill's eyes gleamed, "Ye could do that?"

Sir Justin smiled and struck a posture: "Come test your strength against the might of Roaring Bill, the greatest fighter in England. Like Hercules, he showed his strength in his cradle. I shan't say he strangled two serpents . . . but he knocked his nurse across the room. Bill's first professional bout was with a pet of the fancy—trained by the great Gentleman Jackson himself. He won the match in two minutes..." Sir Justin paused. "I imagine I could carry on in such a vein for at least a quarter of an hour."

"Eh, you talk good..." Bill grinned. "But are ye sure..."

"To save a lady in distress, I think I have no choice." Sir Justin smiled down at Bessie.

"Oh, that... that be so good of you," she flung her arms around him, giving him a hearty kiss on the lips.

His black eyes glinted, "Careful, my girl, I might want to keep you here."

She gave him a provocative smile, "Shouldn't mind stayin' 'twasn't for Joe."

It was teasing, badinage, banter, harmless, meaningless, Livia told herself—no use to think of it as anything more serious—ridiculous to wish that she could hit Bessie, blacking both of her bold eyes, pull out her golden hair in large handfuls, kick her shins... Livia shrank from contemplation of these primitive, never-experienced emotions—never until now. She was breathing hard, she knew it. She had to turn aside, for fear her seething angers might be visible to several naked eyes. Then, she started and cringed away as Bessie, pouncing on her, hugged her warmly.

"Blest if I 'aven't thanked you. Twas brave o' you to face them two 'ellions all by yourself, little lad."

"Aye, 'twas that," Bill agreed.

"Very brave, my lad," Sir Justin approved.

Livia flushed and stared at the floor, "It wasn't

anything," she mumbled. Their compliments embarrassed and, at the same time, pained her. She had the unwelcome suspicion that Sir Justin was not play-acting—that he had actually taken to thinking of her as a boy, too. Or, if not as a boy, certainly he did not regard her as a desirable woman—how could he? But had anyone ever thought of her that way? Had she ever wanted anyone to think of her in such a manner? A memory of her stubborn emphasis upon her intellectual attainments flitted through her mind. She had stressed them to the blotting out of all other attributes. Indeed, so determined had she been to demonstrate her superior intelligence that she had given precious little thought to her other needs. She had, she remembered, thought Lord Ormond handsome but it had been their conversations which had pleased her—she had felt no stirring of the pulses. Well, she amended, she had felt a slight stirring—but nothing to that which she experienced while in the company of Sir Justin . . .

"Oliver, lad, best come with me, now." Sir Justin said.

She blinked up at him. He had opened the door to the caravan, and meeting his friendly but detached gaze, Livia could have wept.

Seven

"Roaring Bill ... a Bristol Lad, born but two doors away from Tom Cribb ... Cribb it was who floored the mighty Jem Belcher and went on to become the champion of England and Cribb it was who gave young Bill Pickett his first lessons in the fine art of pugilism as perfected by Jim Broughton ..." Sir Justin paused and ran a hand through his hair, now plastered against his forehead. His face glistened with perspiration, the back of his red vest was patched with it and his shirt clung damply to his arms.

Watching him, Livia felt a deep admiration for him. He had been talking extemporaneously for the last twenty minutes but his manner was unruffled and his expression reflected no hint of the strain under which he was laboring. She knew he must be edgy, for the crowd, which was growing larger by the minute, was restless. Bob Baker, the weedy youth who had identified himself as referee and holder of the money box, had cast more than one anxious glance in the direction of the caravan.

"'E's takin' 'is time, 'e is," he muttered to Livia.

"He'll be along in a minute," she whispered back.

"I 'ope so. 'Tisn't like 'om to 'old back. Ain't sick is 'e?"

"Not a bit of it. He'll be here presently," Livia assured him.

"Where be Roarin' Bill," a man yelled from the crowd.

"Maybe 'e's scared," answered another.

"Aye," a pugnacious-looking young man stepped to the side of the ring. "More'n one so-called champeen's met 'is match in Lancaster."

"'Ear, 'ear . . ." roared a large segment of the crowd. "Ain't easy to down a Lancaster lad."

"May'ap 'e turned tail'n runned," suggested someone else.

"Now, gentlemen," Sir Justin smiled. "You know that anything good's worth waiting for . . ."

"'Ow long?" the pugnacious young man demanded.

"Aye, 'ow long . . ." echoed some members of the crowd.

Livia cast a glance back toward the caravan. She saw nothing, but since Bill might not be coming from that direction, it did not matter. She glanced at the crowd—all of them were men and while there were several well-dressed individuals among them, most seemed to hail from the fields. They were a rough lot and she could imagine what would happen if Bill didn't show soon.

"'Nother minute'n they'll be rushin' the platform," Bob Baker grimaced. "I never knowed 'im to . . ." he broke off with a long sigh of a relief, and staring straight in front of him, he said, "Ah, there 'e be."

Following his gaze. Livia saw Bill elbowing his way through the crowds and let out a breath she did not even realize she had been holding. In another second, he had climbed up between the ropes to join Sir Justin in the ring.

Smiling broadly, Sir Justin stepped forward, "Is there anyone present who dares to challenge the great Roaring Bill Pickett, champion of champions, one of the finest pugilists in all England? Five pounds and a fight to the finish!"

There was a chorus of acquiescence as a number of burly youths pushed forward jostling each other to get to the side of the ring and glaring at each other so ferociously that it seemed as if they might strike each other down before they even had a chance at the champion.

"'Old it . . . 'Old it," leaning on the ropes, Bill laughed. "Leave one of you for me . . ."

"I'm first . . ." growled one.

"No, I am . . ." yelled a huge beefy man.

"It's me as was 'ere afore you . . ."

"No, me."

"Will ye 'old it," Bill entreated. "I'll take ye all on but one at a time."

"Mightn't 'ave the time if'n it's me . . ." said the huge beefy man, pushing forward to ringside.

Looking at him, Livia saw that his shoulders were immense and his face bore signs of surviving more than one battering. He was easily a stone heavier and a head taller than Roaring Bill. Livia shot a nervous glance at Sir Justin. Though she failed to catch his eye, she was momentarily reassured by the lack of concern with which he regarded the challenger.

"Your name, sir." he asked politely.

" 'Sir,' is it?" the huge man guffawed. " 'Tis Dan Macklin, *Sir*." He cast a look around the assembly and winked.

"Very well, Macklin, come up and put your money in the box," Sir Justin said crisply. "The champion will match it."

Macklin climbed into the ring followed by a small, shabby man with a pale face and furtive eyes. "This 'ere's my cousin, Sir," Macklin pointed at his champion. " 'E'll second me'n supply the blunt."

"Put it in 'ere," Bob Baker held up the box.

" 'Ere . . ." Bill dropped some coins into the box and the small shabby man followed his example, caressing each coin as though he were loath to let it go.

Moving to his corner, Bill shed his jacket and shirt. A murmur of approval ran through the crowd as they looked upon powerful biceps and a broad chest tapering down to a slim waist. There was. however, an even louder murmur as Macklin stripped to reveal a torso so muscular that it seemed that he must possess the strength of an unshorn

Samson. Beside that mighty frame, Bill appeared a mere pygmy.

Livia cast another glance at Sir Justin and again she found him looking marvelously unconcerned. Remembering that he had been wearing that precise expression during those tense moments before Bill had put in an appearance, her spirits drooped. She should have guessed that he would never reveal his true feelings, particularly at such a time.

Baker had stepped forward and was saying something, but she hardly heeded him. She was far too distressed over Bill's inevitable fate. In the crowd, they were laying bets as to the outcome of the match—it seemed to Livia that she could hear Dan Macklin's name repeated far more often than that of Roaring Bill. Obviously the spectators agreed with her. "'E's a Lancashire Lad, 'e is," someone yelled." Others chimed in until it became a chant.

"Go at 'im Lancashire Lad . . . at 'im . . . at 'im."

The two men were facing each other. Tensely, Livia watched as they stepped forward. Baker was speaking to them but she could not hear what he was saying—the chanting of the crowd was too loud.

Macklin and Bill closed in on each other and Livia thought she had never seen anything as terrible as the look on Macklin's ugly countenance as he confronted Bill. His expression was savage, bestial— while Bill seemed as calm as ever. She longed to close her eyes, but she dared not—a boy would not, nor would he clasp his hands together as she was

145

doing. She hastily separated them and dug them into her pockets, shuddering as a spectator yelled, "Gi' it to 'im on the sneezer."

"On 'is knowledge-box—knock 'is brains out," screamed another.

Similar sentiments were roared out from a dozen throats, but though Macklin made an admirable attempt to land a blow on Bill's nose and another to his head, rushing at the smaller man like the angry bull he resembled, his flailing fists failed to find their target. Bill had stepped nimbly away from that headlong rush and, amazingly, he had landed what someone in the crowd admiringly termed a "regular facer" on his opponent.

"That's drawin' 'is claret," howled another enthusiast as a stream of blood dripped down Macklin's assaulted cheek.

"Go for 'is glimmer, Mack," screamed the challenger's cousin.

With a furious roar, Macklin rushed at Bill again but it was he who staggered back with a half-shut eye. In another few moments, Bill, now the darling of the fickle crowd, had dropped Macklin to the canvas and Sir Justin was helping his snivelling cousin to drag the challenger from the ring.

Glimpsing his gory countenance, Livia felt ill, but it would not do to betray herself to Sir Justin, now climbing back onto the platform with a passing smile and a wink for her. Consequently, she clapped and cheered Roaring Bill, hoping fervently that others might be deterred by Macklin's fate. Of course, it proved to be a vain hope and in a regrettably short time several other challengers had left scarlet trails

146

across the canvas. As she watched, Livia began to perceive a terrible sameness in the matches—crude courage against what was obviously a scientific method of footwork and punching. She wondered why Roaring Bill's opponents could not realize that they stood very little chance against such a master—but they could not. One after the other they came to conquer—only to be pummeled and felled.

Meanwhile, the merciless May sun beat down on her. As the restive crowd pressed close to the ropes, the stench of unwashed bodies filled the air. This, combined with the sounds of legions of buzzing flies, drawn by the scent of spilled blood, made Livia's head ache. The sight of bloodied noses, gashed cheeks, swelling eyes and bruised bodies revolted her. She needed to be away from there; she needed to be cool and quiet. She cast a glance at Sir Justin, wondering if she should communicate her distress. Much to her regret, he seemed as excited as any of the other men in that howling inferno. A second later, she had decided that was all to the good—she did not want him to know she was such a poor-spirited female after all. If she were to leave, he would not even notice her departure.

Sliding down from the platform, she managed to worm her way through the masses of people to the caravan, only to discover that the door had been locked. The sun was burning down on the steps—she could not sit there bathed in its virulent rays. She looked about her desperately and her eyes fell on the tent of the fortune-teller. Sir Justin had ordered her to avoid the gypsies, but still that dark interior promised shade. She dug in her pocket and felt a few coins. She could have her palm read—at least it would give her some surcease from the infernal rumbling of the crowd. Hesitating only a second longer, she went across the grass and slipped inside the tent.

It was not cooler. The heat followed her in—but the light did not. At first, dazzled by the brightness outside, she could see nothing, but in a moment she found herself in a sort of antechamber, furnished with a long bench. A few paces beyond her, semitransparent lengths of material painted with cabalistic signs screened that part of the tent where the seer plied her trade. Evidently, she had a customer, for Livia heard a low, murmuring voice. She moved toward the bench and came to a stop, putting her hand to her head. There was a throbbing in her temples. It seemed to her that it was increasing, traveling from her head to the hollow between her collar bones and from there to her whole body—a steady beat, a drumbeat, pounding, pounding and the darkness was growing, encroaching upon her until with a little frightened moan, she felt herself falling into it.

Wetness and a pungent taste on her tongue, a stream of some liquid trickling down her throat, brought her to consciousness. Livia coughed, gagged slightly and swallowed convulsively. Opening her eyes, she saw a dark face above her—a face that flickered and twinkled before her misty eyes. In a moment, she realized it was not the face that was flickering but the light from a candle held over her. The taste on her tongue was brandy and it burned in her throat.

"Feelin' better little one?" the face ceased to

flicker, the light having been steadied, placed on something. The voice was soft, a woman's voice. Memory, springing back into her brain informed her that it must be the fortune-teller. "I . . . swooned," she whispered, adding, "I . . . I've never swooned before."

" 'Twas the heat and all, little lady," the woman soothed.

"Oh," Livia groaned, realizing that in her confusion she had neglected to use her Oliver voice. "I . . ." her hand stole down to her breeches but explanations trembled into silence on her tongue. She did not know what to say.

" 'Tis best not to talk, little lady. Lie you here until you've a mind to be up'n about."

"My . . . uncle, he will be looking for me . . ." Livia felt her face heat up as she looked into the fortune-teller's eyes. They were dark, even darker than those of Sir Justin. Though the candle flame gave her no very clear picture of them, she had the odd conceit that they penetrated through flesh, through bone, into the very workings of her brain so that the woman was well aware that she was no lad and the man with whom she was traveling was no relation. Even as those thoughts were occurring, she felt her hand being lifted. The woman was holding it near the candle flame and peering at the palm.

" 'Tis best ye do not try to find your uncle. 'Tis best ye do not leave this tent. Aieee." The clutch on Livia's hand tightened as the sigh fanned her cheek bringing with it a faint oniony scent. "There is much you *ought* to do, little lady, but ye'll not heed me, for the gold must mesh with the black if the pattern's to be complete. An' there's naught I can tell ye save to take care, which ye'll not do, however hard you try."

"I . . . I do not understand you." Livia was filled with vague feelings of alarm.

"Were I to explain, ye'd still not understand nor would ye believe me nor should ye . . . for 'twill be best when you think it worst, best for ye . . . best for him also. An' you must remember this last what I have said." She lowered Livia's hand, placing it gently beside her. "I must leave. There are people waiting for me. Lie here until you've a mind to go, little lady . . ."

"I wish you could tell me," Livia began.

"Ah, but I can tell you nothing more'n I have said . . . only remember that the worst is best. An' it'll not be long in coming. Even now, it's beginning and will not be stopped." She rose.

"I . . . ought to cross your palm with silver," Livia reached into the pocket of her breeches.

"No, 'twas not you that asked . . . 'twas me that told and that is different. I was told to tell and that is different, too. For that I can take no silver." She rose and moved back. "Rest where you are until you are ready to go . . ."

"I should be ready now. You've been so kind." Livia tried to sit up but her head was still light and an uncomfortable whirling sensation followed the movement. "I expect I ought to lie here a little longer. It's so warm outside . . . and the blood . . . It was folly to imagine I could stomach it . . ."

"Aye," the woman nodded, "but 'twill not serve to dwell upon it. Rest."

Livia's eyelids were heavy. "He'll wonder where I am," she said drowsily.

"And will find you."

"He said I wasn't to . . ." she began and realized she could not tell the women about Sir Justin's stipulations but, in that same moment, she found herself alone. The woman had moved very softly, she thought, like a ghost. It added to the sense of unreality that was invading her or, if not unreality, detachment centering in the back of her head. She expected that it was a residue of her swoon. It must be, for she had never experienced it before, nor had she ever swooned before.

She smiled wryly. Marianne had once told her that swooning was very effective on certain occasions. "When you have seen something horrid or said something you oughtn't and there's no graceful way of getting out of it, giddiness or a swoon answers very well. You must needs be graceful about it though." Marianne had demonstrated a slow descent to the floor. "It is much better, however, to be near enough to a gentleman that he must catch you or else look like a great fool!" Livia's wry smile underwent a natural progression into a bitter laugh. Her own swoon had certainly been a waste—conducted in private with none about to catch her and productive only of a prediction about the best being worst or the worst being best, which did not seem to mean anything. She had a vision of a swooning Marianne in Sir Justin's arms. He would not have failed to catch her and her golden curls would have spilled over his arm—that was an image that brought Bessie to mind. The glances he had bestowed upon

Bessie had been full of admiration. Did she remind him of Marianne . . . Livia grimaced, she had much in common with Marianne—she was a cheat and a liar. And, what had the gypsy meant about the best and the worst? It hardly mattered because the enlightened mind rejected prediction as mere superstition and . . . Livia's eyes closed and she fell into a deep sleep.

She awakened with a start. A spate of conversation close to her ear had left the sound of words echoing through her head. Though she did not know what had been said, there had been an urgency about them and a tone. The tone brought Sir Justin to mind. He must be talking in his sleep again. She sat up and was, for a moment, frightened and confused—for certainly she was not in their tent. However, in another second, she remembered that she had fallen asleep in the fortune-teller's tent. Stumbling to her feet she gazed about her—seeking the entrance. It was darker inside than it had been when she came in and the entrance was not immediately discernible. Finally, she found it and slipped out, looking about her in some dismay. The sun was lower in the sky—it must be close on four in the afternoon—possibly even later. The bouts would be at an end.

A hand fell on her shoulder. An incipient cry of fright died in her throat as she looked up and, to her relief, found Sir Justin at her side. He was breathing hard and he carried his vest over his arm. His shirt, unbuttoned to the waist, hung open over a chest wet with perspiration. "You . . . where have you been?" he panted. "I have been searching everywhere for you . . . everywhere . . . Where did you go?"

She gestured at the tent behind her. "I was in there. You see I ..."

"In there!" His angry shout drowned her explanations. "Is that where you were all this time? Having your damned fortune told?"

"No, I ..."

Unheeding, he continued. "I was combing the fairgrounds for you ... I thought ..." Grabbing her by the shoulders, he glared down at her. "Can you imagine what you've put me through ... I told you you were not to go in there ..." he shook her.

"D-Don't ... please ... let me explain ..."

"Explain what? Explain that you deliberately disobeyed me ... sneaking in there ... you deserve a good beating!"

"I did not sneak," she retorted, her own anger rising. "How d-dare you s-speak to me like this ... you ... you've no right ..." Wrenching herself out of his grasp, she sped away from him, running blindly down the path between the tents, dodging around people, running until she was brought up short by someone who planted himself directly in her path.

"'Ere wot's this?" a man grunted.

She tried to slip around him only to be caught by the arm and held firmly while her captor growled, "It's 'im."

Livia, looking up at him, gasped and a pulse began to beat heavily in her throat as she recognized one of the brothers whom Bessie had cheated. He was Bert, the uglier of the pair. His hard hands dug into her arms and, meeting his lowering glance, she was seized with panic. "Let me go!" she cried.

"Not so fast," Tom, the other brother, had joined them. "Yer right. 'Tis the lad wot was sittin' on the steps o' the caravan ... 'im wot 'adn't seen 'er ... damn liar."

Livia made another futile effort to free herself, "Let me go," she panted.

"Them wot tells lies deserves to be punished," Bert stated. "Them wot says someone's not there'n she is there'n she's 'elped to get away by 'is master ... deserves to be punished so's they won't do it again, ain't that right, Tom?"

"Right as rain." Tom agreed.

Confronted by their sullen brutish faces, Livia's fear increased but it would not do to let them see it. She needed to be clever. "Wot was I to do?" she cried. "I'd've been beaten if I'd told you the truth. You saw Bill ... 'twasn't my doin' ... I said wot I 'ad to say ... wot I were told to say."

"That's the way of it, eh?"

"That be true an' 'is 'ands're 'ard ..." she put a bit of a whine into her tone. "You seen 'im."

"Aye, we seen 'im ... leadin' our gal away after we paid four pound for 'er ... four pound an' naught to show for it." Tom snarled. " 'Twere a bad turn 'e done us."

"Aye'n one bad turn deserves another, eh, brother?" Bert suddenly grinned.

Livia tensed. They were planning something—she was sure of it. Something that involved her, she was sure of that, as well. "P-Please, I didn't ... 'ave nothin' to ... to do wi' it," she whined.

"No, ye did just as ye were told," Bert's grin widened. "An' that's 'ow it should be when ye're 'ired to work for a body. We come 'ere today to find us a boy for our farm ... Ye're a mite small but I expect ye could do yer share ..."

"N-No, I ... I be 'ired out to B-Bill for a year ..." she protested out of a mouth grown suddenly dry.

"Do 'ee pay you four pound a year?"

"Not bloody likely," Tom chuckled. "Take more'n one year to work out that sum ... an' we might as well take it outa 'is 'ide ... 'e owes it to us, rightly. Lad, ye 'ear that? Yer comin' wi' us." Moving to Livia's side, he seized her arm in his hard grasp while Bert, loosening his hold on her shoulder, took her other arm. "Might as well start for 'ome ... wouldn't want to run into 'is master ..."

She felt weak with terror. "No, ye can't ... B-Bill's my m-master, ye c-can't ..." Seeing a young couple walking near them, she struggled in the grasp of her captors crying out, "Help ... Help ..."

The man turned and stared, "Wot's amiss."

" 'Tisn't nothin'," Bert growled. "This 'ere lad ... caught 'im wi' 'is fingers in my pocket ... an' we're takin' 'im to the constable ..."

"It's not true ... they're a-abductin' me ..." Livia sobbed. "My master's R-Roarin' Bill ..."

"An' lies as easy as 'e steals ... c'n you see this lad apprenticed to a pugilist ... when 'e couldn't swat a fly? It's goin' to be gaol for 'im'n maybe transportation."

"It's not true, oh, believe me that it's not," Livia shrilled but to no avail. The young man, evidently sizing up the muscular strength of the two men, drew conclusions which would apply to his own safety and turned away, rejoining the indignant girl who waited for him.

Bert's hand was gripped around her shoulder, the fingers digging deep into her flesh. "Now, ye listen to me, younggun," he said in a savage undertone. "Ye sing out like that again an' I'll knock yer teeth down yer throat'n break yer nose besides."

"You . . . you ain't got no right to t-take me," she dared to say.

"An' did yer fine master 'ave any right to steal our Bessie wot we paid four pound for? You ain't much of an exchange for 'er, but we'll need to make do . . . so come on quietlike or by 'eaven, I'll split yer face for ye . . ."

Words crowded onto her tongue, pleas, threats and the truth trembled there and were stilled by the ferocious glare Bert bent upon her. There was nothing that could sway him from his purpose. Telling the truth would be the most dangerous ploy she could use, dangerous in ways at which she, remembering Bessie's stricken face, could only guess. She cast one glance between them at the crowds. If only she might see a pursuing Sir Justin and call out—but, of course, she did not. In her erratic dash between the tents, she had done as she had intended and lost him—and in losing him had lost herself as well. Bert's hand was clamped upon her shoulder and Tom's paw was heavy on her arm. The proximity of her captors, the sight of their heavy faces and hard eyes filled her with terror—she had to get away. She moved restively and winced as Bert's cruel hold tightened. She could not get away. Hopelessly, she bowed her head and submitted to being taken where they would.

• • •

Out of nowhere, a number of large clouds had appeared upon the western horizon so that, rather than quitting an unblemished sky, the sun was descending amidst streaks and blots of a brilliant gold-tipped orange. A cool wind had sprung up, setting the flags and pennants atop the billowing tents to fluttering. Silhouetted against the brilliant sky, it was a sight to make more than one person stop and exclaim over its beauty. However, Sir Justin, striding in the direction of Bill's caravan, was in no mood to appreciate a view which, on another occasion, must have appealed mightily to him. He had been searching for Livia and, as earlier in the day, had not found her. He could only hope that she had made her way back to Bill's caravan—but there was a nagging fear in his mind that told him she had not. It was more than a fear—it was a premonition of danger such as he had experienced at odd times during his life and on each occasion he had been right. His lips twisted. It was part of his inheritance from his damned grandmother. He shook his head, not wanting to think of her—never wanting to think of her and the old days when he . . . when she . . . No, he must banish her and her sayings from his thoughts, forget the premonitions else he would be no better than the scurvy tinkers and the horse copers, who roamed the byways of his country and were hated for very good reason.

Inhaling a long breath, he expelled it as a weighted sign. In banishing his grandmother and her ilk, he had opened his mind to other equally unwelcome thoughts concerning his own actions. The furies which had possessed him when, after a long and wearisome search through the fairgrounds, he had found that Livia had been sequestered in the fortune-teller's tent, had died down to be replaced by an emotion relatively new to him—self-reproach. He had treated her badly—shaking her as if she were indeed his disobedient little nephew. His reaction had been all out of proportion to the deed. That she had not heeded his stipulations concerning the gypsies was hardly surprising—she could not know the truth and he should have remembered that all females were inclined to visit palmists, tea-leaf readers and stargazers. His grandmother and her people were well aware of that and through the ages they had profited mightily from that unfortunate weakness.

He remembered Livia's halting efforts to explain, to placate him, and he wished he had listened, but he had not listened, he had reacted only to his own anger. He wondered where she had gone and a slight, unwilling smile played about his lips. One would not have thought that a female could have been so nimble, dodging and wheeling around the tents and through the crowds like a boy, a frightened, shaken boy. He bit his lip and glared at the ground. He must have been mad to treat her in such a manner and though it was, and had ever been, damned hard for him to make apologies, he must make them to her. It was only that he had come to think of her as his special charge—his nephew? No, not quite. A memory of the previous night, when he had awakened to find her kneeling beside him, holding him, was enough to bring a dark flush to his cheeks—her little hands had been so gentle on his arms. He had other memories of her, too, none of which held her to be anything but female. Furthermore, she had been so brave and uncomplaining. He winced, thinking of her bloodied heels. Then, there had been the fights. He frowned. He never should have let her witness them. It was no place for a gently bred young woman—a side glance at her had told him she must be sick as a cat. He had not been surprised to find her gone—he had only been worried that he had not found her, and then to see her right in his path, his relief had been well-nigh overwhelming—and what had he done? He could not continue to dwell on that—to upbraid himself for that which had passed. He had to find her. He quickened his steps—she was in either the tent or the caravan. Even given her hurt and her own anger, she would not want to remain out on the grounds after sunset. She must be there—his fear that she might not be . . . his sense of an impending danger . . .

She was not in the tent. He moved to the caravan and upon entering found Bill with a tankard of ale in his hand—looking marvelously fit for one who had spent several grueling hours taking, as well as giving out, the blows that had netted him enough guineas to make it more than worth his while.

"I been wonderin' where you was," Bill favored him with a cheerful grin. "'Ave a drink wi' me, man. I vow if I don't think yer twice as good as Arthur was . . ."

Sir Justin broke in hastily, "You . . . you've not seen my nephew?"

"No, 'e's not been 'ere. Bent on pleasurin' 'im-self at the booths, still, no doubt. 'Ee ..." he broke off, looking over Sir Justin's shoulder. " 'Ere wot do you want?" he demanded in some surprise.

Turning, Sir Justin saw the fortune-teller standing just below the steps. He started forward. "Is my nephew with you, then?" he demanded hopefully.

She shook her head. "I've been hoping you'd've been back before this, my cousin," she said in her own language. "You must be on your way quickly, quickly."

Unmindful of Bill, he responded in the same tongue, the tongue his grandmother had taught him in his cradle, "He is in danger?"

"Aye, in bad danger ... she's been taken ..."

"Taken where and by whom?" he hurled the words at her.

"My brothers can describe them ..."

"Where can your brothers be found?"

"Come, they await you." She moved into the shadows.

He leaped after her down the steps and, as he did, he heard Bill call after him—but he could not stop to answer. All his fears had returned to plague him and judging from the look in his cousin's eyes, the peril was even greater than he had feared.

Eight

Pulled by a pair of sturdy horses, the farm cart lumbered over the uneven roads. It was a cumbersome vehicle with a seat for its two drivers and room for either produce or passengers under its raised canvas top. This particular cart was piled high with sacks of grain and fertilizer. Its one passenger, securely bound and gagged, lay amidst the sacks. The ropes were tight and bit into her flesh, her mouth was dry and her terror was such that she thought she must die of it. They had been traveling for what seemed hours. She was sure it must be near eight in the evening, for it had been easily an hour since the cracks in the canvas had shown her a glimmering of daylight.

From such snatches of conversation as she had

overheard, she knew they were nearing their destination. Then what? They would find out the truth about her—it would be inevitable, she knew it; knew, too, that she would be facing the peril that had threatened Bessie, Bessie who had inadvertently brought this trouble upon her. She could not blame the girl. She, Livia Pemberton, was to blame for all that had happened to her since her ill-starred decision to follow Lord Ormond to Gretna Green.

If ... but she could not continue to mull over the series of sorry happenings that had culminated in her present predicament—one from which she saw no possible means of extricating herself! She would be the victim of those two terrible young men, whose ugly laughter had occasionally seared her ears as one or the other had mockingly inquired if she were comfortable back there.

If she could offer them money, if she could explain ... but they would never credit her explanations. She was at their mercy, they who had proven that they had no mercy. She would never see Sir Justin again, but he did not want to see her! He had been so angry ... no, not angry, worried, she knew that now ... concerned because he had not been able to find her and disturbed because she had gone to the gypsy's tent. She swallowed a lump in her throat ... poor Sir Justin. If only she could have assured him that it did not matter—that mixture of blood which appeared to give him such distress—but he would not know the truth from her. She would never see him again—never, never, never. Fool—she had been so foolish to run away from him, but she had been hurt, too, loving him as she did. The lump would not be swallowed and there was no checking the tears that rolled down her cheeks. He would never know of her love—but it would not matter, for he did not love her, but at least he did not dislike her anymore. If they had been allowed to go on together . . . perhaps . . . but it was futile to dwell upon "ifs" and "perhaps," because it was over, finished. Her journey was at an end. . . . One of Shakespeare's wise fools—Feste of *Twelfth Night*—had sung "journeys end in lovers meeting." Her lover would be Death. She shuddered. Once her captors had done with her, she would crave nothing else. She would be no better than those hapless women who roamed the purlieus of Covent Garden and whose bodies were regularly fished from the Thames and buried in potter's field.

"If I could die now . . . before anything happens . . . before I am ravished . . ." She was not sure of the meaning of the word. Vaguely, she knew those women of Covent Garden had been ravished, had suffered "the fate that was worse than death," but she was not sure what it entailed. She had once asked Miss Sims what it meant, only to be sternly reprimanded for "curiosity unbecoming to a female." However, she was positive that it concerned some manner of hurt inflicted by a man. Another shudder shook her—to be near Bert and Tom was hurt enough—to have felt their hard hands on her flesh and to remember Bert saying to his brother, " 'E's got skin soft as any woman's, 'E needs toughenin', 'e does."

"Aye'n us'll see 'e gets it," Tom had loosed one of his ugly laughs.

To die at their hands . . . she hated to give them that satisfaction. If she could free herself from her bonds—but she had tried and tried—to no avail. With all her frantic efforts, she had succeeded only in rubbing her wrists raw. No, escape did not lie that way but... she tensed. She had heard the sound of horses; several, she thought, and coming from behind. If she might cry out or in some way make her presence known. There was a chance she could knock her head against the canvas but it was dark now and no one would see that movement, and even if they did see it, they would probably think the men were carting some animal. Still, she made an effort to move, but though she managed to roll over, the sides of the cart were too high for her to succeed in touching the canvas. The sound of hooves was loud in her ears—there were three, perhaps four horses. They galloped quickly past the cart, the beat of their hooves resounding on the road and then diminishing in the distance. More tears rolled down her cheeks. There was nothing she could do—nothing save resign herself to the inevitable.

"'Oo were they?" Tom muttered. "Looked a proper set o' clinkers, they did."

"Aye," Bert returned, "eh, wot's this?" his voice rose in anger and the cart seemed to shudder, dislodging some of the sacks of produce as it came to a jolting stop.

"Wot're they doin' blockin' the road?" Tom growled furiously.

The riders must have stopped! Livia wondered why. Perhaps, if she could attract their attention... but the gag was so tightly tied. Was there a way to ease it off? She rubbed her face against the sacks but, again, it was a futile effort. They had trussed her expertly—she was as powerless as a market-bound goose.

Muttered blasphemies filled her ears, "Wot do ye want?" Bert yelled.

"Get down from there," came the curt command.

Livia started. It was his voice . . . Sir Justin's . . . no, how could it be? She must be growing light-headed.

"Bloody 'ighwaymen, where be the pistol?" Tom whispered.

"Ere . . ." Bert said.

He was reaching for it. He would shoot. Livia threw herself against the seat.

"Damn ye wot're ye about?" Bert's fist descended but only grazed her cheek as she rolled out of reach.

"Get down!"

It *was* Sir Justin's voice. She could not be mistaken. Then, she cowered as a shot rang out. It had been fired at such close range that she was momentarily deafened. Her nostrils were filled with the acrid stench of gunpowder but she hardly heeded it. Her heart was pounding. Her whole body was throbbing with fear. Had the bullet struck Sir Justin? Scarcely daring to breathe, she listened and then suddenly the seat shook as if a heavy weight had fallen upon it and the wagon jerked forward.

Cursing loudly, Tom yelled, "'Ere you get off . . ." his cry was strangled in his throat and a second later there was a heavy thud, followed by a yell from Bert.

"Tom . . . get away wi' ye, damn ye . . . Tom, man . . . Blast ye, lemme go, I say . . ." It was Bert and evidently he was fighting with someone ... someone who might have leaped upon the seat.

The horses neighed wildly. Bert cried out and once more the wagon started forward. Livia was tossed back and forth as it came to another jarring stop that dislodged more bags of grain—one of which fell across her face. She tried to lift her head and throw it off but she could not move. She could not breathe! She moaned deep in her silenced throat and in that moment the sack was pulled away and she saw the gleam of a lantern just above her head. It must have been held by a hand that was shaking, for its beam danced crazily over the fallen sacks and, in another moment, she was trying to shrink away from a flame which was perilously close to her face.

"Livia, thank God ... thank God ..." Sir Justin cried in a voice that was oddly husky. The lantern was thrust back and someone must have seized it, for he was using both hands to pull away the sacks and, then, in a voice that shook with anger, he cried, "Oh, my God, the ropes ... they are so tight. Damn them ... damn them to hell."

Reaching down, he lifted her out of the wagon. Then, holding her against his chest, he carried her across the road and put her down gently on a clump of grass. He ripped the gag from her mouth. "Did they hurt you much ..." he asked, still in that strange husky voice.

She tried to speak but no words would come. Sobs shook her.

"Oh, my dear ..." producing a long knife, he slit her bonds. "Oh, God," he murmured, touching her scraped wrists, "Poor child ... poor child ..."

A moon brighter than any lantern illuminated his face and with a little moan Livia threw herself against him, clutching him tightly and burying her head against his chest. "You came . . . you came . . ." she murmured. "I did not think that I . . . I should ever see you again . . . I was so f-frightened . . . so f-frightened . . . I . . ."

His hand was in her hair, stroking it, "Shhh, shhh, you must not cry . . . you are safe . . . my dear . . . they cannot harm you now . . . we have them." There was an undercurrent of anger and of something else, which she did not identify until he said, "They . . . did not . . . abuse you in any way . . ."

She flushed and shook her head, "They . . . did not guess the . . . the truth."

His arms tightened about her, "Thank God," he said brokenly. "If they'd touched you . . . I should have strangled them . . . I would I might even now . . . those beasts . . . and the ropes so tight . . ." he stroked her wrists. "This was my fault . . . all mine. If I'd not spoken as I did . . . and shaken you . . . believe me, I did not mean it . . . I was only . . ."

"Hush," she said. "It's not true . . . it was not your fault . . . you could not know I should encounter them . . . You were angry and worried. I understood . . . and it doesn't matter . . . you are here . . ."

"You cannot have understood my anger," he said in a low troubled tone. "It had naught to do with you . . . it was part of my denial of something I should not have denied or refuted. Because of that, you've suffered needlessly . . . needlessly. When I saw you near my cousin's tent . . ."

"Your 'cousin' . . . ?"

"My cousin." He repeated in a harsh voice. "She

is Rosa . . . a Lovell . . ." he broke off as a young man hurried forward, speaking quickly in the language Livia now recognized as Romany.

Smiling grimly, Sir Justin answered in the same tongue and, turning back to Livia, he said with just a shade of defiance, "This is Rosa's brother, Anselo . . . my cousin Anselo . . ." he waved a hand. "Over there among the trees with your erstwhile captors are my cousins Tubal and Tawno Lovell. They're the ones to whom you owe your freedom. It was they who saw you being abducted and it was Tawno, who, out of a regard for me that I little deserved, discovered the way they were going and spread the word that others of the Romany folk should watch as well . . . There are eyes in many hedgerows along this route and they were well observed. We knew of every turn you took . . ."

"Oh," Livia looked up shyly at the gypsy. "I do thank you, sir."

"'Tis naught," the young man smiled at her. Turning back to Sir Justin, he added, "Tawno take care of them?"

Sir Justin turned to Livia, "My cousins believe it best to truss the brothers up in the same manner that you were tied, put them in the back of the wagon and give the horses their heads."

"But would that not be very dangerous? I—I'd not have them—maimed or killed."

"You are kinder than they deserve. But I think they'll take little harm from the ride. The animals will find their way back to the stable in their own good time . . . it might take the rest of the night."

Livia's eyes gleamed. "Oh, if that is true, I've no objection. It would be most fitting, I think."

"Not fitting enough," he told her. He addressed a few words to his cousin, who grinned, nodded and hurried away. Turning back to her, Sir Justin added, "If you're wondering how we are related . . . my grandmother was also a member of the Lovell tribe."

She stared at him wide-eyed, "And that's the heritage you'd deny?"

He looked away from her, "It cannot surprise you, can it? Gypsy blood might be a proper ingredient for a witches' brew, but it's not for the veins of gentlefolk . . . as was often pointed out to me in my youth."

She had an instant and vivid image of the sensitive boy he must have been and knew she had been right in her contention that those who knew of his heritage had not scrupled to hurt him. She said gently, "You cannot believe that."

"You do not?" his look was challenging.

She returned his look steadily, "I should consider it . . . Indeed, I do consider it the spice that has improved the blend."

There was a moment of silence as he stared into her eyes, "Either you are being kind . . ."

"Not 'kind.' Honest."

"Livia, my dear." Reaching for her hand, he held it clasped in both of his. She had never heard so gentle a note in his voice, "I must tell you that . . ." but whatever he had meant to say was cut off by a sudden shout from down the road. Releasing her hand, he rose and, turning in that direction, he called back. Then, reaching down, he pulled her to her feet. "Come," he smiled. "It's time to bid your fine friends a long farewell."

A few moments later, Livia stood with Sir Justin watching the farm cart go bumping down the lane drawn by a pair of horses whose rumps had been smartly thwacked. The sacks of produce had been removed and divided among the trio of gypsies and she imagined that Bert and Tom, lying tightly bound and helpless in its rough and splintered bottom, would have more than one cause to regret their removal. Yet, though she had joined with Sir Justin and his cousins in laughing over a retribution that was not only swift but eminently just, she had not felt like laughing. It seemed to her that before he had been interrupted, Sir Justin had been on the verge of saying something very meaningful . . . but there was no use to dwell on it—for while he was being far more gentle with her than had been his wont, the feel of . . . could she call it—intimacy—that she had experienced, or imagined she had experienced . . . was gone.

Sitting on the caravan steps, Livia stared at the square lineaments of Carlisle Castle on its distant hill. It had stood on that particular eminence for more than seven centuries. Sir Justin had taken her there in the early morning. He had also shown her the ruins of an ancient Roman fort; he had been equally informative about Penrith, where they had been the previous day and where they had visited Preston Moor, where one hundred seventy years earlier, Cromwell had skirmished with the forces of King Charles I. These historical sites might have fascinated her a week ago—but, at present, she could scarcely remember what she had seen—for she had been far more aware of him, of his nearness.

She was yet reveling in the moments when he had found it necessary to take her hand and, as had happened when he had shown her the fort, to lift her in his arms. She heaved a long sigh. Nearly three days had passed since her ordeal and most fortuitous rescue, and on the morrow, Sir Justin, having completed his work for Bill Pickett, would take her back to London.

"Nor shall we need to go by stage," he had told her. "My cousins, who could have helped us earlier, have advanced the monies for the hire of a post chaise. They may look like raggle-taggle beggars, but they have their sources." He had sighed. "I've been a fool . . . but no matter, I've learned the error of my ways."

She could agree on that. In the last three days, a subtle change had come over him. He seemed freer—more inclined to jest—and the somber look which had been evident in his eyes was gone, at least most of the time. Yet, she was cognizant of a constraint between them and once or twice, on looking up, she had caught him staring at her. She sighed again. Impossible to read his mind . . . impossible to guess what might happen once he took her back to London. They had yet to concoct a tale to satisfy her relations—but that did not matter. What mattered was—their pending separation. Would he want to see her again—afterwards? Her heart seemed to be pounding in her throat . . . not to see him again, not to be with him . . . it was something too terrible to contemplate. Indeed, it was impossible to imagine not being with him. Last night, lying in the tent, she had listened as long as she could to the sound of his breathing and the thoughts that had arisen were, again, far from those which should have existed in the mind of a properly brought-up young female—but she could no longer include herself in those ranks. In the short time she had known him—another Livia had emerged—a woman, passionate and wanting. One who loved him and craved his love and longed to tell him so. It was not pride that stilled her tongue. She had no pride. It was not even the fear of rejection—it was the fear that he might, in view of the compromising nature of their situation, feel himself obliged to offer for her. That would be terrible. Again, she thought of that moment when he had said, "I must tell you that..." and had been interrupted. "That what?" What had he wanted to tell her and why had that confidence not been forthcoming at a later time ...

"Livia."

Startled, she looked up to find Sir Justin standing not two feet away. "Oh, I ... did not see you ..."

"No," he smiled at her. "Your gaze was bent upon the ground. Evidently, you were deep in thought. Might I offer you a penny for those thoughts?"

"You'd have the worst of the bargain," she said and was pleased because her tone sounded so casual, so light. "Are the bouts at an end, then?"

"Yes ... and our Bill borne off to the tavern with such challengers as could still stand erect. He wanted me to fetch you that we might lift a glass with them—but I've a mind to see more of this territory before we must leave it. There's a fragment of Hadrian's Wall just beyond the River Sark ... who knows—we might even meet up with your

172

ghostly centurion. Should you like to come?"

"The Sark . . . is that not at the Scottish border?"

"It is the Scottish border. Had we gone to Gretna Green, we'd have crossed it and taken the road for Dumfries . . ."

"Gretna Green . . ." she murmured and looked at him incredulously. "Can you believe that I . . . I had not connected Carlisle with it . . ."

There was a gleam of laughter in his dark eyes, "Then I am to take it that the hole in your heart that was labeled 'Ormond' has been quite sealed over?"

"I am beginning to think it never existed. Indeed since I . . ." she hesitated and felt her cheeks grow warm.

" 'Since' what?" he prodded.

She did not look at him. She did not dare. What would his reaction have been had she finished that sentence . . . since I have known you, since I have loved you, since . . . it was well she had remembered that she was not thinking, she was speaking. "Since I have c-come here . . . I have been more interested in the town of Carlisle," she improvised. "The—c-castle and the cathedral and the city walls . . ."

" 'The city walls'?" he repeated. "I thought we'd agreed they were uncommonly filthy and would be the better for a thorough cleaning?"

"But still interesting . . ." she persevered.

"I am glad you are interested in walls . . . for that means you will find that which Hadrian built even more to your taste."

"I am sure I shall."

"Then . . . come, we must hire a post chaise or a curricle . . ." he held out his hand.

As she clasped it, Livia felt a strange vibration which she had experienced on other occasions but never so strongly. It seemed to her as if a flame had been ignited between them, and wondered if he might not have experienced it, too. However, on looking at him, she failed to catch his eye. He only repeated, "Come . . . our drive will be a long one."

She bit down a sigh. She had never been less anxious to visit a Roman wall . . . but at least there was some consolation in the fact that she would be viewing it with him. Dolefully, she wondered how many more times she would be able to rejoice in his company before . . . but she would not dwell on that . . . she would live in the present and in his presence.

Since neither post chaise nor curricle had been available, Sir Justin had settled somewhat disdainfully for a gig and a far from mettlesome steed. Dun-colored and long of tooth, it answered to the improbable appellation of Pegasus, though the landlord of the inn from whence it came explained that it had long ago been shortened to Peg. None of the names that Sir Justin conferred upon the animal during the two hours it took them to reach the Sark bore any resemblance to either Pegasus or Peg.

It was soon borne upon Livia that he was in a very odd humor. While at the beginning of the drive he had punctiliously indicated points of interest along the route, he had gradually lapsed into a frowning silence punctuated with thunderous frowns as he exhorted Pegasus to "Giddup, damn you . . . lift those flat feet!" However, once they had approached a very narrow stream which wound its

174

sluggish way between flat, treeless banks and which, to Livia's surprise, proved to be the River Sark, her companion's smiles returned and he looked upon that inferior trickle with far more appreciation than she felt it deserved.

Livia was willing to agree that the portion of Scotland that lay directly up the hill from the river was pleasant enough. Pegasus, for once given free rein by Sir Justin, ambled along roads bordered by cornfields and by broad stretches of green pastureland thronged with woolly black-faced sheep and which broke into hilly distances covered with yellow flowers for which she had no name. She imagined that somewhere on that broad expanse of land lay the wall they were seeking. She was sure of it when Sir Justin, reaching into his pocket, took out a small guidebook and consulted it.

"Are we nearing it?" she asked as he put it away.

"What?" he demanded.

"The wall . . ."

"'The wall?' He looked at her quizzically and then he smiled. "Oh, yes, soon."

Shortly after they had reached the top of the hill, the road narrowed and the scenery grew less felicitous. They entered a small village which contained a number of very ugly houses, all depressingly similar and giving the impression of having been built by an architect with no eye to a family's comfort. She was glad when they left the village behind —but they soon came into another hamlet which, while it had the promise of ancient trees and one rather pleasant-looking inn, proved upon closer inspection to have houses no more prepossessing in appearance than those they had seen in its sister village. There were, however, quite a few carriages, curricles and post chaises drawn up in the dreary portion of land which, Sir Justin informed her, was the town square, and where on finding a place to secure the gig, he drew rein.

"We're stopping here?" she asked.

"Yes ... we have arrived at our ... destination, madame."

"'Our destination,'" she repeated. "The wall ..."

"Not the wall. This village, my dear, is Gretna Green."

"Gretna Green!" she exclaimed, staring at him confusedly.

"Yes ... it's not a very prepossessing place."

"No ... but ... I do not understand ..."

"Has it not always been our destination?" he asked.

Her heart sank. "You ... still hope that Marianne ... but that could not be p-possible ... they could not be still here!"

"No," he smiled, "I cannot imagine that anyone would want to remain here once they had completed that for which they came," he agreed.

"Then ... why?"

"Should you not like to see it ... I should think that all you have heard about it—must whet your curiosity. I must confess that I am highly interested in watching a blacksmith officiate at a wedding ceremony. Doubtless it is not only more rewarding but considerable easier than shoeing a horse."

She stared at him. "Are you ... serious?"

"Never more."

"It . . . it will not give you pain to . . . watch."

"'Pain'?" he raised his eyebrows. "Why should it?"

"Marianne," she said in a small voice.

"'Marianne'!" he suddenly laughed. "No . . . 'tis a wound that left no scar." He sobered. "But I think I must tell you why . . . You have been kind enough to assure me that my . . . heritage does not disturb you . . ."

"It was not kindness . . . it was the truth . . . believe me," she said gently.

His eyes softened, "I believe you and am more grateful than I can tell you. Your uncle was of a similar mind . . . However, years ago . . . when I was barely twenty, I offered for the daughter of a neighboring family and was told by her father that I was not acceptable because of my connections . . ."

"Oh, Sir Justin . . ." she breathed. "How cruel."

He shrugged. "It was nothing more than I'd expected. My mother, too, rejected me. She was like unto Marianne in coloring . . . blonde, blue-eyed, fair of skin . . . when I was no more than three, I knew she did not like to look upon me . . . or my father. When I was four, my father was killed in a hunting accident and my mother married again less than six months later. She left me with my grandmother . . . Until the day of her death . . . two years ago, I did not see her."

"Oh . . . but why did she marry your father, then?"

"Money," he said harshly. He was wealthy . . .

177

she, a curate's daughter, was poor but beautiful and beguiled him into believing that she loved him. My grandmother told me the truth of it, but I'd not believe it. Somehow when I met Marianne . . . I was reminded of my mother . . . and she appeared to like me . . . that meant a great deal to me . . ."

"And then she ran away from you . . . It must have seemed as if . . . oh, Justin, I am so sorry." Livia's eyes filled with tears.

"No matter," he said gently. "As I told you . . . she means nothing to me anymore . . . and has not for days. I only wanted you to know the way of it." He had grown very sober and he looked at her with a mixture of intensity and uncertainty. "Livia, I fear I have not been quite frank with you this afternoon . . . you see I had it in mind to ask you a question the other night. Then, we were interrupted and I thought the time not right. Perhaps it is still not right. Perhaps I am mistaken in a certain belief that I have come to hold . . ." he paused and seemed to swallow some manner of obstruction in his throat and cleared it. "Miss Pemberton . . . I know we did not meet under the most felicitous of circumstances. We were much at odds in the beginning, but I must tell you that since I have come to know you, my respect for you has grown with each passing hour. It is not only respect that I feel—it is admiration for your courage. I can think of no other female—with possibly the exception of my grandmother, whom I did love, for all I . . . but never mind that. I can think of none else who would have suffered the trials we have undergone together with such fortitude." He hesitated, then in a lower voice, he continued, "I fear, however, that I have been very high-handed in my actions of this day. Let me explain that they have arisen out of my very great regard for you and from the strain of being with you and . . ."

" 'The s-strain'?" she repeated.

He flushed, "I am not making myself clear, I fear. I know what I wanted to say . . . but it has occurred to me that I have put the cart before the horse. Certainly I should have asked, then acted. Damn it all, Miss Pemberton . . . Livia, I love you and I have brought you here to this benighted spot because I cannot remain in your company another hour . . . another minute unless we are wed. And if I am not . . ."

"Sir Justin," Livia cried. "I pray you will say no more. I cannot bear it."

His face fell, "You are telling me that you do not reciprocate . . ."

She bounced toward him and flinging her arms around his neck, she cried joyfully, "I am saying that you did not have to tell me a half of what you just said . . . a sentence, a word would have sufficed. I am saying that I love you so much . . . so entirely that . . ." she paused as Pegasus, evidently startled by her sudden movements, backed up and reared, trumpeting forth his indignation in a loud whinny. While Sir Justin hastily soothed him, Livia burst into laughter, adding, "Pegasus must be of the opinion that I, too, am talking far too much. I beg you will you tie this wise animal to that post and let us be wed without further ado."

"Livia . . ." With total disregard for those drivers who still remained in their vehicles, Sir Justin drew her into his arms, but then he released her almost immediately and, reaching inside his coat, he brought out a large parcel. "This is for you, my love."

"For me?"

He nodded and, tearing it open, he took out a simple cotton gown. "I should have preferred to give you silks and satins ... and shall do ... along with pearls and diamonds, my dearest—but meanwhile, considering our momentarily straitened circumstances, this must suffice ..."

"But you did not need to buy me a gown ..." she murmured.

"Oh, but I did ... for even here, I think it must not seem as if I were wedding my nephew."

The room was high and low. That is to say that its location was high—at the very top of the inn Livia had seen as they had driven into the village of Gretna Green—and its ceiling was low. The furnishings were scant—a battered armoire, a table on which was a chipped china ewer in a much mended basin, a small night table, and the bed, a venerable four-poster, the mattress of which was thin and old. However, the sheets were clean and the bride, lying between them, found her present accommodations a definite improvement over the makeshifts of the past fortnight. However, she was not really thinking very much about the chamber or its furnishings, for the door had just opened and a long flame-cast shadow had fallen across the bed.

"Oh, Justin ..." she breathed happily.

"My dear love?" he asked in a tone that sent all manner of thrills coursing through her body.

"I am so very happy."

The bed sent forth a creaking groan as he sat down at its edge. "I am, too, my love."

"I can hardly believe we are wed . . ."

"I intend that you shall believe it and soon . . . though I cannot say much for our 'minister.' "

"Do not criticize him," she reprimanded. "I thought him beautiful."

" 'Beautiful'!" he scoffed. "An unshaven reprobate who smelled strongly of spirits, gabbled the ceremony as if he were running a race with himself and who loosed a stream of spittle at the floor directly he had pronounced us 'Man and Wife.' "

"He was beautiful," she insisted. "And I am glad he spoke so quickly. Oh, Justin I have loved you for such a long time."

"No longer than I have loved you."

"I cannot believe that. You hated me in the beginning."

"Never."

"You were certainly not attracted to me," she accused.

"On the contrary, I became attracted to you . . . even before I began to love you."

"I cannot believe it."

"Can you not, my Aphrodite?"

" 'Aphrodite'?" she repeated. "Why would you call me so?"

He had set the candle on the table near the bed but its gleam remained in his eyes, "Perhaps I should not tell you . . ." he smiled.

"You must."

"Aphrodite . . . was born in the waters."

She stared at him perplexedly. "I do not understand you."

"I was thinking of a certain pool in a copse on the road to Preston."

Livia sat up and glared at him, "You'll never tell me that . . . that you *looked!*"

"Of course I looked," he admitted, moving closer to her and dropping a kiss on her bare shoulder.

"Sir . . . you are no gentleman!"

"Fortunately, not, my dearest love, else I should have been denied a glimpse of what I do not hesitate to term . . . perfection."

She flushed, "You are wicked, sir . . . wicked and utterly reprehensible."

"I admit it freely, my beautiful one . . . and I fear you cannot know how much more wicked and reprehensible I mean to be before this night is at an end."

Moving toward him, Livia twined her arms around his neck, clinging to him rapturously, the while she whispered in his ear, "Of course, I cannot, but I am in hopes that you will soon show me, my dearest Justin."

Epilogue

On a morning toward the end of May, a carriage drawn by four matched grays and boasting two postilions as well as two footmen made its way up the long driveway that lay beneath towering beeches. Their destination was a most remarkable edifice which looked to be half-castle, half-cathedral, and the whole, unmistakably Gothic, in a style that Horace Walpole of Strawberry Hill fame would have approved. Square of outline and covered with ivy, its roof was crenelated and, at intervals, crowned with small stucco turrets, which by their newness, gave the impression of having been stuck there as an afterthought. A huge round tower and a high peaked tower gave much the same impression, while to the left of the whole was an ancient Norman keep of undoubted authenticity. Stained-glass windows flanked a recessed doorway and the whole facade was punctuated by windows which by their shape suggested the decorated period so popular in fourteenth-century churches.

A few paces from the door, the equipage rolled to a stop. One of the footmen hastened to bring out a pair of stairs for the convenience of the passengers, while the other footman opened the carriage door. He stood back respectfully as a tall young woman, garbed in the height of fashion, emerged into the sunlight. As she moved, her light summer cloak fell back from her shoulders to reveal a magnificent pearl necklace clasped about her slender throat. A diamond ring above a plain gold band glistened on the hand she placed on the footman's arm. Immediately upon reaching the ground, she turned solicitously to watch as the footmen assisted an elderly man down the steps and handed him his cane. The young woman hurried to take his arm and was rewarded with a warm and loving smile for her pains. Behind them, yet another passenger was assisted from the coach—a young woman, also clad in the height of fashion, though without the jewelry worn by the first lady. Once she had alighted, she stared up at the mansion and frowned but the expression hardly marred her very beautiful face.

The elderly man stepped up to the massive door and was about to seize a large dragon-shaped knocker, when the door swung open. "Ah, your Lordship," a black-clad butler smiled a welcome. "Will you come in?"

"Thank you, Elveston." His Lordship, standing back, allowed his fair companions to precede him.

Once inside, the ladies glanced about them in awe at an immense paneled hall containing highly polished suits of armor—at maces, lances and swords attached to the walls and at hanging red and green banners emblazoned with a white and gold family crest. Unlike the house, the furnishings of the hall looked to be authentically ancient and an immense oaken table was certainly medieval.

"Will your Lordship care to wait in here? I shall inform Sir Justin that you have come," the butler said, indicating an arched doorway.

"Of course," his Lordship replied.

The trio moved into a drawing room and the two women gasped in unison—then, for some reason, they glared at each other and turned aside to admire the chamber separately.

It was truly magnificent. In keeping with the Gothic design of the castle, its ceiling was a fantasy of molded plaster, while the sun, streaming through a stained-glass window, threw a pattern of multicolored squares and circles upon furnishings which had been purchased during the late Egyptian craze. This was notable for settees with serpentine and crocodilian ornamentation, for sphinx-borne tables and for singularly stiff and uncomfortable-looking chaise longues. A huge mirror stretching up from a caryatid carved marble mantelpiece reflected the whole room, including several of the fine Italian and Flemish Renaissance oils which hung on walls of scarlet damask. The floor was covered with a fine Oriental carpet.

His Lordship allowed the effect of this chamber to sink in before he said to the stylishly clad young girl at his side, "Sit down my dear."

She obeyed at once and, indicating another chair, she said shyly, "And you, too, must sit down, my Lord."

His Lordship seemed glad to accede to this request and, looking at the other girl, he said with a slight frown, "Come, my dear, stop prowling about and compose yourself."

The beauty ignored him and continued to move about the room, gazing at the paintings and at various fine objets d'art upon the tables and in a pair of cabinets. Suddenly, she said nervously, yet hopefully, "Can you think that he has actually forgiven me, Papa?"

"I cannot imagine that he would have included you in this invitation if he had not, Marianne. Once I had written to him concerning your disappointment and disillusionment in that scoundrel Ormond, his answer was most sympathetic and understanding. Though certainly you do not deserve such generosity after all the havoc you have wrought upon him and your poor cousin Livia. For a while I feared that she might have put a period to her existence until your Aunt Maude told me that she was in seclusion at Riversedge."

"I wrote to her and I explained all. I told her she had a fortunate escape from that . . . that rogue," Marianne's eyes flashed. "I begged her to forgive me."

" 'Twas not enough," murmured the other girl.

Marianne whirled on her, glaring at her, "I will thank *you* to keep your unsolicited opinions to yourself!" she snapped.

"And I will thank you not to address your stepmama in that disrespectful manner," said Lord Semple in equally acrimonious tones as he patted his wife's hand gently.

"If you imagine that I will ever acknowledge..." Marianne began freezingly but broke off, quickly arranging her features into a welcoming smile as their host strode into the room.

Seeing him, Marianne bit back a gasp. Wearing a loose silk shirt with a rolling Byronic collar, light buckskin breeches thrust into riding boots, and with his black locks falling into waves over his brow, no one would ever have mistaken him for a country parson—he looked amazingly handsome. Yet the change in him, she thought, was not limited to his appearance. His manner had altered, too. He did not seem so stiff nor so unapproachable. Falling into a low curtsey, Marianne murmured, "Dear Sir Justin," with a look in which admiration, shyness and penitence were artfully blended.

"Miss Semple," he smiled at her cordially and becoming forward bore her hand to his hips.

However, it was to be noted that he was equally cordial to Lord Semple and to the young woman who was introduced as Lady Semple.

Pleasantries having been dutifully exchanged, Sir Justin said, "I am indeed pleased to see that you have recovered from your injury so quickly, Lord Semple."

"I have had excellent nursing," his Lordship explained with a grateful look at Lady Semple. "I must say that you are looking extremely fit... in spite of all the vicissitudes you mentioned in your first letter."

"I feel myself the better for them, sir. But please, you must come into the garden."

"Oh, I do love a garden," Lady Semple enthused.

Sir Justin opened the hall door, "I hope that this one will meet with your approbation, Lady Semple."

"I . . . am sure it must, sir," she told him shyly.

"The gardens of Warre are rightly famous, my love," Lord Semple smiled at his wife.

Escorting Lord and Lady Semple into the hall, Sir Justin waved a hand at an archway through which streamed brilliant sunshine. "They are directly through there and . . ."

"Sir Justin," Marianne moved forward, "a moment, I beg you."

"Of course, Miss Semple," he turned toward her while Lord Semple escorted his lady through the archway.

"I pray you'll not continue to call me 'Miss Semple' in that odious way," she murmured, putting her hand on his arm and looking up at him out of beseeching blue eyes. "Not after all we have been to each other. Oh, I know you will say that I played a scurvy trick on you and it's true. There can be no refining on that . . ."

"Miss . . . er, Marianne," he began uncomfortably.

"Please hear me, I . . . I must tell you . . . that I knew very soon that I had been sadly beguiled." Her eyes flashed, "We had not gone a hundred miles before I discovered he was quite impossible . . . an arrant fortune hunter. Again, I shall not refine upon my sufferings. Suffice to say that I discovered the error of my ways before . . . anything untoward had taken place. I left him as soon as I might . . . I hope never to look upon his face again . . ." she broke into an angry little laugh, perilously close to a titter. "I imagine I shall not need to . . . since I understand he has been clapped into the Fleet Prison for debt!" Her anger vanished and she wrung her hands, "It . . . was a t-terrible experience. He misled me completely as to his . . . as to everything. I can only say that I found out in time." She looked down and fluttered her long lashes.

"I'm sorry that it did not turn out as you had hoped, Miss . . . Marianne."

"You are kind . . . very kind to want to see me again. Oh, Justin, I am the most miserable of females. You see what took place in my absence. I cannot live with Papa and with that creature he has wed . . . and upon whom he lavishes jewels and . . . oh, it is not to be borne! And Papa tells me you have forgiven me." She regarded him uncertainly, "Is that really the truth?"

"It is really the truth," he affirmed. "Indeed, my dear Marianne, I consider myself very much in your debt."

"In *my* debt," she repeated. "I do not understand you."

"Come into the garden, my dear, and I shall explain the whole of it." He held out his arm.

Taking it, she smiled up at him, saying softly, "Justin, my dear, cannot we pretend that all this never happened?"

He gave her a long look, "I do not believe we can do that, Marianne."

Her eyes clouded, "Then . . . you . . . you've not forgiven me at all . . ." she said with a tiny sob.

"Oh, but I have," he insisted and moving a little more briskly than she would have preferred, he led her into the garden. She gasped and her hold on his arm tightened as a peacock which had been strolling near the door as they emerged, hissed, and extending its long neck in a singularly serpentlike movement, backed out of her way.

"Do not be afraid," Sir Justin smiled. "Sometimes these birds do not respond as you think they might, given their great beauty—but you will find that they are quite harmless."

"I am glad of that," Marianne said and forthwith forgot the peacock's bad manners as she stared about her to clipped yew hedges, marble statuary and myriads of red, yellow, white and purple tulips. "How very lovely . . ." she murmured appreciatively.

"Not anymore," he said. "The tulips are at an end, but the roses are blooming. I shall show you." He led her toward what appeared to be the ruins of a small medieval church, half covered by vines. However, upon approaching it, she saw that it was a folly set with stone benches encircling a round pool covered with lavender and white water lilies. Seated on one of the benches was Lord Semple, looking, Marianne thought, both surprised and pleased. Near him, Lady Semple was talking excitedly with another young woman. Marianne could see only the back of her head which she noted, somewhat to her amusement, was covered with very short, riotously curling brown hair—a style that had gone out at least ten years earlier. However, despite the odd haircut, she could see that her summer muslin gown was new and in the very latest style.

Her stepmother's excited tones drifted back to

her and she winced as she heard her say, "An' so you see, I recovered first'n was able to 'elp 'im. The old woman they'd got from the village, she were tipsy most o' the time'n 'twas easy to see she didn't know the first thing 'bout carin' for a body. 'E were feelin' ever so poorly'n I sat wi' 'im an' did wot I could to make 'im comfortable. An' well, you see ... M-Miss ... er, Milady ... er ..."

"Livia, my dearest Nancy," the young woman said. "And I am delighted. I truly am. My congratulations to you both."

"L-L-Livia," Marianne gave Sir Justin a terrified glance. "Oh, no, what is s-she doing h-here? I daren't face her ... I daren't ..."

"But of course you can, my dear Marianne." Placing his hand beneath her elbow, Sir Justin propelled her forward to Livia, who was, she noted with some anger, looking very beautiful and far more radiantly happy then any jilted and forsaken bride had a right to look. "I am sure you will be pleased to know, Marianne," Sir Justin continued, "that my wife has also forgiven you, have you not, my love?" Releasing Marianne, he stepped to Livia's side and rested his hand caressingly upon her shoulder.

"Oh, yes," Livia smiled at her dumbfounded cousin, "of course I forgive you ... with all my heart."

Unconsciously echoing Sir Justin, she said, "Indeed, I find myself much in your debt." She reached up to touch her husband's hand. "And I am delighted you have come so that I might thank you in person, Marianne."